Ballads by William Makepeace Thackeray

The great author of Vanity Fair and The Luck Of Barry Lyndon was born in India in 1811.

At age 5 his father died and his mother sent him back to England. His education was of the best but he himself seemed unable to apply his talents to a rigorous work ethic.

However, once he harnessed his talents the works flowed in novels, articles, short stories, sketches and lectures.

Sadly, his personal life was rather more difficult. After a few years of marriage his wife began to suffer from depression and over the years became detached from reality. Thackeray himself suffered from ill health later in his life and the one pursuit that kept him moving forward was that of writing. In his life time, he was placed second only to Dickens. High praise indeed.

Index of Contents

BALLADS

THE CHRONICLE OF THE DRUM

PART I

At Paris, hard by the Maine barriers,
Whoever will choose to repair,
Midst a dozen of wooden-legged warriors
May haply fall in with old Pierre.
On the sunshiny bench of a tavern
He sits and he prates of old wars,
And moistens his pipe of tobacco
With a drink that is named after Mars.

The beer makes his tongue run the quicker,
And as long as his tap never fails,
Thus over his favorite liquor
Old Peter will tell his old tales.
Says he, "In my life's ninety summers
Strange changes and chances I've seen,—
So here's to all gentlemen drummers

That ever have thump'd on a skin.

"Brought up in the art military
For four generations we are;
My ancestors drumm'd for King Harry,
The Huguenot lad of Navarre.
And as each man in life has his station
According as Fortune may fix,
While Condé was waving the baton,
My grandsire was trolling the sticks.

"Ah! those were the days for commanders!
What glories my grandfather won,
Ere bigots, and lackeys, and panders
The fortunes of France had undone!
In Germany, Flanders, and Holland,—
What foeman resisted us then?
No; my grandsire was ever victorious,
My grandsire and Monsieur Turenne.

"He died: and our noble battalions
The jade fickle Fortune forsook;
And at Blenheim, in spite of our valiance,
The victory lay with Malbrook.
The news it was brought to King Louis;
Corbleu! how his Majesty swore
When he heard they had taken my grandsire:
And twelve thousand gentlemen more.

"At Namur, Ramillies, and Malplaquet
Were we posted, on plain or in trench:
Malbrook only need to attack it
And away from him scamper'd we French.
Cheer up! 'tis no use to be glum, boys,—
'Tis written, since fighting begun,
That sometimes we fight and we conquer,
And sometimes we fight and we run.

"To fight and to run was our fate:
Our fortune and fame had departed.
And so perish'd Louis the Great,—
Old, lonely, and half broken-hearted.
His coffin they pelted with mud,
His body they tried to lay hands on;
And so having buried King Louis
They loyally served his great-grandson.

"God save the beloved King Louis!

(For so he was nicknamed by some,)
And now came my father to do his
King's orders and beat on the drum.
My grandsire was dead, but his bones
Must have shaken I'm certain for joy,
To hear daddy drumming the English
From the meadows of famed Fontenoy.

"So well did he drum in that battle
That the enemy show'd us their backs;
Corbleu! it was pleasant to rattle
The sticks and to follow old Saxe!
We next had Soubise as a leader,
And as luck hath its changes and fits,
At Rossbach, in spite of dad's drumming,
'Tis said we were beaten by Fritz.

"And now daddy cross'd the Atlantic,
To drum for Montcalm and his men;
Morbleu! but it makes a man frantic
To think we were beaten again!
My daddy he cross'd the wide ocean,
My mother brought me on her neck,
And we came in the year fifty-seven
To guard the good town of Quebec.

"In the year fifty-nine came the Britons,—
Full well I remember the day,—
They knocked at our gates for admittance,
Their vessels were moor'd in our bay.
Says our general, 'Drive me yon redcoats
Away to the sea whence they come!'
So we marched against Wolfe and his bull-dogs,
We marched at the sound of the drum.

"I think I can see my poor mammy
With me in her hand as she waits,
And our regiment, slowly retreating,
Pours back through the citadel gates.
Dear mammy she looks in their faces,
And asks if her husband is come?
—He is lying all cold on the glacis,
And will never more beat on the drum.

"Come, drink, 'tis no use to be glum, boys,
He died like a soldier in glory;
Here's a glass to the health of all drum-boys,
And now I'll commence my own story.

Once more did we cross the salt ocean,
We came in the year eighty-one;
And the wrongs of my father the drummer
Were avenged by the drummer his son.

"In Chesapeake Bay we were landed.
In vain strove the British to pass:
Rochambeau our armies commanded,
Our ships they were led by De Grasse.
Morbleu! How I rattled the drumsticks
The day we march'd into Yorktown;
Ten thousand of beef-eating British
Their weapons we caused to lay down.

"Then homewards returning victorious,
In peace to our country we came,
And were thanked for our glorious actions
By Louis Sixteenth of the name.
What drummer on earth could be prouder
Than I, while I drumm'd at Versailles
To the lovely court ladies in powder,
And lappets, and long satin-tails?

"The Princes that day pass'd before us,
Our countrymen's glory and hope;
Monsieur, who was learned in Horace,
D'Artois, who could dance the tightrope.
One night we kept guard for the Queen
At her Majesty's opera-box,
While the King, that majestical monarch,
Sat filing at home at his locks.

"Yes, I drumm'd for the fair Antoinette,
And so smiling she look'd and so tender,
That our officers, privates, and drummers,
All vow'd they would die to defend her.
But she cared not for us honest fellows,
Who fought and who bled in her wars,
She sneer'd at our gallant Rochambeau,
And turned Lafayette out of doors.

"Ventrebleu! then I swore a great oath,
No more to such tyrants to kneel.
And so just to keep up my drumming,
One day I drumm'd down the Bastille.
Ho, landlord! a stoup of fresh wine.
Come, comrades, a bumper we'll try,
And drink to the year eighty-nine

And the glorious fourth of July!

"Then bravely our cannon it thunder'd
As onwards our patriots bore.
Our enemies were but a hundred,
And we twenty thousand or more.
They carried the news to King Louis.
He heard it as calm as you please,
And, like a majestical monarch,
Kept filing his locks and his keys.

"We show'd our republican courage,
We storm'd and we broke the great gate in,
And we murder'd the insolent governor
For daring to keep us a-waiting.
Lambesc and his squadrons stood by:
They never stirr'd finger or thumb.
The saucy aristocrats trembled
As they heard the republican drum.

"Hurrah! what a storm was a-brewing:
The day of our vengeance was come!
Through scenes of what carnage and ruin
Did I beat on the patriot drum!
Let's drink to the famed tenth of August:
At midnight I beat the tattoo,
And woke up the Pikemen of Paris
To follow the bold Barbaroux.

"With pikes, and with shouts, and with torches
March'd onwards our dusty battalions,
And we girt the tall castle of Louis,
A million of tatterdemalions!
We storm'd the fair gardens where tower'd
The walls of his heritage splendid.
Ah, shame on him, craven and coward,
That had not the heart to defend it!

"With the crown of his sires on his head,
His nobles and knights by his side,
At the foot of his ancestors' palace
'Twere easy, methinks, to have died.
But no: when we burst through his barriers,
Mid heaps of the dying and dead,
In vain through the chambers we sought him—
He had turn'd like a craven and fled.

"You all know the Place de la Concorde?

'Tis hard by the Tuilerie wall.
Mid terraces, fountains, and statues,
There rises an obelisk tall.
There rises an obelisk tall,
All garnish'd and gilded the base is:
'Tis surely the gayest of all
Our beautiful city's gay places.

"Around it are gardens and flowers,
And the Cities of France on their thrones,
Each crown'd with his circlet of flowers
Sits watching this biggest of stones!
I love to go sit in the sun there,
The flowers and fountains to see,
And to think of the deeds that were done there
In the glorious year ninety-three.

"'Twas here stood the Altar of Freedom;
And though neither marble nor gilding
Was used in those days to adorn
Our simple republican building,
Corbleu! but the MERE GUILLOTINE
Cared little for splendor or show,
So you gave her an axe and a beam,
And a plank and a basket or so.

"Awful, and proud, and erect,
Here sat our republican goddess.
Each morning her table we deck'd
With dainty aristocrats' bodies.
The people each day flocked around
As she sat at her meat and her wine:
'Twas always the use of our nation
To witness the sovereign dine.

"Young virgins with fair golden tresses,
Old silver-hair'd prelates and priests,
Dukes, marquises, barons, princesses,
Were splendidly served at her feasts.
Ventrebleu! but we pamper'd our ogress
With the best that our nation could bring,
And dainty she grew in her progress,
And called for the head of a King!

"She called for the blood of our King,
And straight from his prison we drew him;
And to her with shouting we led him,
And took him, and bound him, and slew him.

'The monarchs of Europe against me
Have plotted a godless alliance
I'll fling them the head of King Louis,'
She said, 'as my gage of defiance.'

"I see him as now, for a moment,
Away from his jailers he broke;
And stood at the foot of the scaffold,
And linger'd, and fain would have spoke.
'Ho,drummer! quick! silence yon Capet,'
Says Santerre, 'with a beat of your drum.'
Lustily then did I tap it,
And the son of Saint Louis was dumb."

PART II

"The glorious days of September
Saw many aristocrats fall;
'Twas then that our pikes drunk the blood
In the beautiful breast of Lamballe.
Pardi, 'twas a beautiful lady!
I seldom have looked on her like;
And I drumm'd for a gallant procession,
That marched with her head on a pike.

"Let's show the pale head to the Queen,
We said—she'll remember it well.
She looked from the bars of her prison,
And shriek'd as she saw it, and fell.
We set up a shout at her screaming,
We laugh'd at the fright she had shown
At the sight of the head of her minion;
How she'd tremble to part with her own.

"We had taken the head of King Capet,
We called for the blood of his wife;
Undaunted she came to the scaffold,
And bared her fair neck to the knife.
As she felt the foul fingers that touch'd her,
She shrunk, but she deigned not to speak:
She look'd with a royal disdain,
And died with a blush on her cheek!

"'Twas thus that our country was saved;
So told us the safety committee!
But psha! I've the heart of a soldier,
All gentleness, mercy, and pity.

I loathed to assist at such deeds,
And my drum beat its loudest of tunes
As we offered to justice offended
The blood of the bloody tribunes.

"Away with such foul recollections!
No more of the axe and the block;
I saw the last fight of the sections,
As they fell 'neath our guns at Saint Rock.
Young BONAPARTE led us that day;
When he sought the Italian frontier,
I follow'd my gallant young captain,
I follow'd him many a long year.

"We came to an army in rags,
Our general was but a boy
When we first saw the Austrian flags
Flaunt proud in the fields of Savoy.
In the glorious year ninety-six,
We march'd to the banks of the Po;
I carried my drum and my sticks,
And we laid the proud Austrian low.

"In triumph we enter'd Milan,
We seized on the Mantuan keys;
The troops of the Emperor ran,
And the Pope he tell down on his knees.—
Pierre's comrades here call'd a fresh bottle,
And clubbing together their wealth,
They drank to the Army of Italy,
And General Bonaparte's health."

The drummer now bared his old breast,
And show'd us a plenty of scars,
Rude presents that Fortune had made him,
In fifty victorious wars.
"This came when I follow'd bold Kleber—
'Twas shot by a Mameluke gun;
And this from an Austrian sabre,
When the field of Marengo was won.

"My forehead has many deep furrows,
But this is the deepest of all:
A Brunswicker made it at Jena,
Beside the fair river of Saal.
This cross, 'twas the Emperor gave it;
(God bless him!) it covers a blow;
I had it at Austerlitz fight,

As I beat on my drum in the snow.

"'Twas thus that we conquer'd and fought;
But wherefore continue the story?
There's never a baby in France
But has heard of our chief and our glory,—
But has heard of our chief and our fame,
His sorrows and triumphs can tell,
How bravely Napoleon conquer'd,
How bravely and sadly he fell.

"It makes my old heart to beat higher,
To think of the deeds that I saw;
I follow'd bold Ney through the fire,
And charged at the side of Murat."
And so did old Peter continue
His story of twenty brave years;
His audience follow'd with comments—
Rude comments of curses and tears.

He told how the Prussians in vain
Had died in defence of their land;
His audience laugh'd at the story,
And vow'd that their captain was grand!
He had fought the red English, he said,
In many a battle of Spain;
They cursed the red English, and prayed
To meet them and fight them again.

He told them how Russia was lost,
Had winter not driven them back;
And his company cursed the quick frost,
And doubly they cursed the Cossack.
He told how the stranger arrived;
They wept at the tale of disgrace:
And they long'd but for one battle more,
The stain of their shame to efface!

"Our country their hordes overrun,
We fled to the fields of Champagne,
And fought them, though twenty to one,
And beat them again and again!
Our warrior was conquer'd at last;
They bade him his crown to resign;
To fate and his country he yielded
The rights of himself and his line.

"He came, and among us he stood,

Around him we press'd in a throng:
We could not regard him for weeping,
Who had led us and loved us so long.
'I have led you for twenty long years,'
Napoleon said, ere he went
'Wherever was honor I found you,
And with you, my sons, am content!

"'Though Europe against me was arm'd,
Your chiefs and my people are true;
I still might have struggled with fortune,
And baffled all Europe with you.

"'But France would have suffer'd the while,
'Tis best that I suffer alone;
I go to my place of exile,
To write of the deeds we have done.

"'Be true to the king that they give you,
We may not embrace ere we part;
But, General, reach me your hand,
And press me, I pray, to your heart.'

"He called for our battle standard;
One kiss to the eagle he gave.
'Dear eagle!' he said, 'may this kiss
Long sound in the hearts of the brave!'
'Twas thus that Napoleon left us;
Our people were weeping and mute,
As he pass'd through the lines of his guard,
And our drums beat the notes of salute.

"I look'd when the drumming was o'er,
I look'd, but our hero was gone;
We were destined to see him once more,
When we fought on the Mount of St. John.
The Emperor rode through our files;
'Twas June, and a fair Sunday morn;
The lines of our warriors for miles
Stretch'd wide through the Waterloo corn.

"In thousands we stood on the plain,
The red-coats were crowning the height;
'Go scatter yon English,' he said;
'We'll sup, lads, at Brussels tonight.'
We answered his voice with a shout;
Our eagles were bright in the sun;
Our drums and our cannon spoke out,

And the thundering battle begun.

"One charge to another succeeds,
Like waves that a hurricane bears;
All day do our galloping steeds
Dash fierce on the enemy's squares.
At noon we began the fell onset:
We charged up the Englishman's hill;
And madly we charged it at sunset—
His banners were floating there still.

"—Go to! I will tell you no more;
You know how the battle was lost.
Ho! fetch me a beaker of wine,
And, comrades, I'll give you a toast.
I'll give you a curse on all traitors,
Who plotted our Emperor's ruin;
And a curse on those red-coated English,
Whose bayonets help'd our undoing.

"A curse on those British assassins,
Who order'd the slaughter of Ney;
A curse on Sir Hudson, who tortured
The life of our hero away.
A curse on all Russians—I hate them—
On all Prussian and Austrian fry;
And oh! but I pray we may meet them,
And fight them again ere I die."

'Twas thus old Peter did conclude
His chronicle with curses fit.
He spoke the tale in accents rude,
In ruder verse I copied it.

Perhaps the tale a moral bears,
(All tales in time to this must come,)
The story of two hundred years
Writ on the parchment of a drum.

What Peter told with drum and stick,
Is endless theme for poet's pen:
Is found in endless quartos thick,
Enormous books by learned men.

And ever since historian writ,
And ever since a bard could sing,
Doth each exalt with all his wit
The noble art of murdering.

We love to read the glorious page,
How bold Achilles kill'd his foe:
And Turnus, fell'd by Trojans' rage,
Went howling to the shades below.

How Godfrey led his red-cross knights,
How mad Orlando slash'd and slew;
There's not a single bard that writes
But doth the glorious theme renew.

And while, in fashion picturesque,
The poet rhymes of blood and blows,
The grave historian at his desk
Describes the same in classic prose.

Go read the works of Reverend Cox,
You'll duly see recorded there
The history of the self-same knocks
Here roughly sung by Drummer Pierre.

Of battles fierce and warriors big,
He writes in phrases dull and slow,
And waves his cauliflower wig,
And shouts "Saint George for Marlborow!"

Take Doctor Southey from the shelf,
An LL. D.—a peaceful man;
Good Lord, how doth he plume himself
Because we beat the Corsican!

From first to last his page is filled
With stirring tales how blows were struck.
He shows how we the Frenchmen kill'd,
And praises God for our good luck.

Some hints, 'tis true, of politics
The doctors give and statesman's art:
Pierre only bangs his drum and sticks,
And understands the bloody part.

He cares not what the cause may be,
He is not nice for wrong and right;
But show him where's the enemy,
He only asks to drum and fight.

They bid him fight,—perhaps he wins.
And when he tells the story o'er,

The honest savage brags and grins,
And only longs to fight once more.

But luck may change, and valor fail,
Our drummer, Peter, meet reverse,
And with a moral points his tale—
The end of all such tales—a curse.

Last year, my love, it was my hap
Behind a grenadier to be,
And, but he wore a hairy cap,
No taller man, methinks, than me.

Prince Albert and the Queen, God wot,
(Be blessings on the glorious pair!)
Before us passed, I saw them not,
I only saw a cap of hair.

Your orthodox historian puts
In foremost rank the soldier thus,
The red-coat bully in his boots,
That hides the march of men from us.

He puts him there in foremost rank,
You wonder at his cap of hair:
You hear his sabre's cursed clank,
His spurs are jingling everywhere.

Go to! I hate him and his trade:
Who bade us so to cringe and bend,
And all God's peaceful people made
To such as him subservient?

Tell me what find we to admire
In epaulets and scarlet coats.
In men, because they load and fire,
And know the art of cutting throats?

Ah, gentle, tender lady mine!
The winter wind blows cold and shrill,
Come, fill me one more glass of wine,
And give the silly fools their will.

And what care we for war and wrack,
How kings and heroes rise and fall;
Look yonder, in his coffin black,
There lies the greatest of them all!

To pluck him down, and keep him up,
Died many million human souls;
'Tis twelve o'clock, and time to sup,
Bid Mary heap the fire with coals.

He captured many thousand guns;
He wrote "The Great" before his name;
And dying, only left his sons
The recollection of his shame.

Though more than half the world was his,
He died without a rood his own;
And borrowed from his enemies
Six foot of ground to lie upon.

He fought a thousand glorious wars,
And more than half the world was his,
And somewhere now, in yonder stars,
Can tell, mayhap, what greatness is.

1841.

This ballad was written at Paris at the time of the Second Funeral of Napoleon.

ABD-EL-KADER AT TOULON. OR, THE CAGED HAWK

No more, thou lithe and long-winged hawk, of desert-life for thee;
No more across the sultry sands shalt thou go swooping free:
Blunt idle talons, idle beak, with spurning of thy chain,
Shatter against thy cage the wing thou ne'er may'st spread again.

Long, sitting by their watchfires, shall the Kabyles tell the tale
Of thy dash from Ben Halifa on the fat Metidja vale;
How thou swept'st the desert over, bearing down the wild El Riff,
From eastern Beni Salah to western Ouad Shelif;

How thy white burnous welit streaming, like the storm-rack o'er the sea,
When thou rodest in the vanward of the Moorish chivalry;
How thy razzia was a whirlwind, thy onset a simoom,
How thy sword-sweep was the lightning, dealing death from out the gloom!

Nor less quick to slay in battle than in peace to spare and save,
Of brave men wisest councillor, of wise councillors most brave;
How the eye that flashed destruction could beam gentleness and love,
How lion in thee mated lamb, how eagle mated dove!

Availéd not or steel or shot 'gainst that charmed life secure,
Till cunning France, in last resource, tossed up the golden lure;
And the carrion buzzards round him stooped, faithless, to the cast,
And the wild hawk of the desert is caught and caged at last.

Weep, maidens of Zerifah, above the laden loom!
Scar, chieftains of Al Elmah, your cheeks in grief and gloom!
Sons of the Beni Snazam, throw down the useless lance,
And stoop your necks and bare your backs to yoke and scourge of France!

Twas not in fight they bore him down; he never cried amàn;
He never sank his sword before the PRINCE OF FRANGHISTAN;
But with traitors all around him, his star upon the wane,
He heard the voice of ALLAH, and he would not strive in vain.

They gave him what he asked them; from king to king he spake,
As one that plighted word and seal not knoweth how to break;
"Let me pass from out my deserts, be't mine own choice where to go,
I brook no fettered life to live, a captive and a show."

And they promised, and he trusted them, and proud and calm he came,
Upon his black mare riding, girt with his sword of fame.
Good steed, good sword, he rendered both unto the Frankish throng;
He knew them false and fickle—but a Prince's word is strong.

How have they kept their promise? Turned they the vessel's prow
Unto Acre, Alexandria, as they have sworn e'en now?
Not so: from Oran northwards the white sails gleam and glance,
And the wild hawk of the desert is borne away to France!

Where Toulon's white-walled lazaret looks southward o'er the wave,
Sits he that trusted in the word a son of Louis gave.
O noble faith of noble heart! And was the warning vain,
The text writ by the BOURBON in the blurred black book of Spain?

They have need of thee to gaze on, they have need of thee to grace
The triumph of the Prince, to gild the pinchbeck of their race.
Words are but wind, conditions must be construed by GUIZOT;
Dash out thy heart, thou desert hawk, ere thou art made a show!

THE KING OF BRENTFORD'S TESTAMENT

The noble King of Brentford
Was old and very sick,
He summon'd his physicians
To wait upon him quick;

They stepp'd into their coaches
And brought their best physick.

They cramm'd their gracious master
With potion and with pill;
They drench'd him and they bled him;
They could not cure his ill.
"Go fetch," says he, "my lawyer,
I'd better make my will."

The monarch's royal mandate
The lawyer did obey;
The thought of six-and-eightpence
Did make his heart full gay.
"What is't," says he, "your Majesty
Would wish of me to-day?"

"The doctors have belabor'd me
With potion and with pill:
My hours of life are counted,
O man of tape and quill!
Sit down and mend a pen or two,
I want to make my will.

"O'er all the land of Brentford
I'm lord, and eke of Kew:
I've three-per-cents and five-per-cents;
My debts are but a few;
And to inherit after me
I have but children two.

"Prince Thomas is my eldest son,
A sober Prince is he,
And from the day we breech'd him
Till now, he's twenty-three,
He never caused disquiet
To his poor Mamma or me.

"At school they never flogg'd him,
At college, though not fast,
Yet his little-go and great-go
He creditably pass'd,
And made his year's allowance
For eighteen months to last.

"He never owed a shilling.
Went never drunk to bed,
He has not two ideas

Within his honest head—
In all respects he differs
From my second son, Prince Ned.

"When Tom has half his income
Laid by at the year's end,
Poor Ned has ne'er a stiver
That rightly he may spend,
But sponges on a tradesman,
Or borrows from a friend.

"While Tom his legal studies
Most soberly pursues,
Poor Ned most pass his mornings
A-dawdling with the Muse:
While Tom frequents his banker,
Young Ned frequents the Jews.

"Ned drives about in buggies,
Tom sometimes takes a 'bus;
Ah, cruel fate, why made you
My children differ thus?
Why make of Tom a DULLARD,
And Ned a GENIUS?"

"You'll cut him with a shilling,"
Exclaimed the man of wits:
"I'll leave my wealth," said Brentford,
"Sir Lawyer, as befits;
And portion both their fortunes
Unto their several wits."

"Your Grace knows best," the lawyer said
"On your commands I wait."
"Be silent, Sir," says Brentford,
"A plague upon your prate!
Come take your pen and paper,
And write as I dictate."

The will as Brentford spoke it
Was writ and signed and closed;
He bade the lawyer leave him,
And turn'd him round and dozed;
And next week in the churchyard
The good old King reposed.

Tom, dressed in crape and hatband,
Of mourners was the chief;

In bitter self-upbraidings
Poor Edward showed his grief:
Tom hid his fat white countenance
In his pocket-handkerchief.

Ned's eyes were full of weeping,
He falter'd in his walk;
Tom never shed a tear,
But onwards he did stalk,
As pompous, black, and solemn,
As any catafalque.

And when the bones of Brentford—
That gentle king and just—
With bell and book and candle
Were duly laid in dust,
"Now, gentleman," says Thomas,
"Let business be discussed.

"When late our sire beloved
Was taken deadly ill,
Sir Lawyer, you attended him
(I mean to tax your bill);
And, as you signed and wrote it,
I prithee read the will."

The lawyer wiped his spectacles,
And drew the parchment out;
And all the Brentford family
Sat eager round about:
Poor Ned was somewhat anxious,
But Tom had ne'er a doubt.

"My son, as I make ready
To seek my last long home,
Some cares I had for Neddy,
But none for thee, my Tom:
Sobriety and order
You ne'er departed from.

"Ned hath a brilliant genius,
And thou a plodding brain;
On thee I think with pleasure,
On him with doubt and pain."
"You see, good Ned," says Thomas,
"What he thought about us twain."

"Though small was your allowance,

You saved a little store;
And those who save a little
Shall get a plenty more."
As the lawyer read this compliment,
Tom's eyes were running o'er.

"The tortoise and the hare, Tom,
Set out, at each his pace;
The hare it was the fleeter,
The tortoise won the race;
And since the world's beginning
This ever was the case.

"Ned's genius, blithe and singing,
Steps gayly o'er the ground;
As steadily you trudge it
He clears it with a bound;
But dulness has stout legs, Tom,
And wind that's wondrous sound.

"O'er fruits and flowers alike, Tom,
You pass with plodding feet;
You heed not one nor t'other
But onwards go your beat,
While genius stops to loiter
With all that he may meet;

"And ever as he wanders,
Will have a pretext fine
For sleeping in the morning,
Or loitering to dine,
Or dozing in the shade,
Or basking in the shine.

"Your little steady eyes, Tom,
Though not so bright as those
That restless round about him
His flashing genius throws,
Are excellently suited
To look before your nose.

"Thank heaven, then, for the blinkers
It placed before your eyes;
The stupidest are weakest,
The witty are not wise;
Oh, bless your good stupidity,
It is your dearest prize!

"And though my lands are wide,
And plenty is my gold,
Still better gifts from Nature,
My Thomas, do you hold—
A brain that's thick and heavy,
A heart that's dull and cold.

"Too dull to feel depression,
Too hard to heed distress,
Too cold to yield to passion
Or silly tenderness.
March on—your road is open
To wealth, Tom, and success.

"Ned sinneth in extravagance,
And you in greedy lust."
("I' faith," says Ned, "our father
Is less polite than just.")
"In you, son Tom, I've confidence,
But Ned I cannot trust.

"Wherefore my lease and copyholds,
My lands and tenements,
My parks, my farms, and orchards,
My houses and my rents,
My Dutch stock and my Spanish stock,
My five and three per cents,

"I leave to you, my Thomas—"
("What, all?" poor Edward said.
"Well, well, I should have spent them,
And Tom's a prudent head.")—
"I leave to you, my Thomas,—
To you in TRUST for Ned."

The wrath and consternation
What poet e'er could trace
That at this fatal passage
Came o'er Prince Tom his face;
The wonder of the company,
And honest Ned's amaze!

"'Tis surely some mistake,"
Good-naturedly cries Ned;
The lawyer answered gravely,
"'Tis even as I said;
'Twas thus his gracious Majesty
Ordain'd on his death-bed.

"See, here the will is witness'd,
And here's his autograph."
"In truth, our father's writing,"
Says Edward, with a laugh;
"But thou shalt not be a loser, Tom,
We'll share it half and half."

"Alas! my kind young gentleman,
This sharing cannot be;
'Tis written in the testament
That Brentford spoke to me,
'I do forbid Prince Ned to give
Prince Tom a halfpenny.

"'He hath a store of money,
But ne'er was known to lend it;
He never help'd his brother;
The poor he ne'er befriended;
He hath no need of property
Who knows not how to spend it.

"'Poor Edward knows but how to spend,
And thrifty Tom to hoard;
Let Thomas be the steward then,
And Edward be the lord;
And as the honest laborer
Is worthy his reward,

"'I pray Prince Ned, my second son,
And my successor dear,
To pay to his intendant
Five hundred pounds a year;
And to think of his old father,
And live and make good cheer.'"

Such was old Brentford's honest testament,
He did devise his moneys for the best,
And lies in Brentford church in peaceful rest.
Prince Edward lived, and money made and spent;
But his good sire was wrong, it is confess'd
To say his son, young Thomas, never lent.
He did. Young Thomas lent at interest,
And nobly took his twenty-five per cent.

Long time the famous reign of Ned endured
O'er Chiswick, Fulham, Brentford, Putney, Kew,
But of extravagance he ne'er was cured.

And when both died, as mortal men will do,
'Twas commonly reported that the steward
Was very much the richer of the two.

THE WHITE SQUALL

On deck, beneath the awning,
I dozing lay and yawning;
It was the gray of dawning,
Ere yet the sun arose;
And above the funnel's roaring,
And the fitful wind's deploring,
I heard the cabin snoring
With universal nose.
I could hear the passengers snorting—
I envied their disporting—
Vainly I was courting
The pleasure of a doze!

So I lay, and wondered why light
Came not, and watched the twilight,
And the glimmer of the skylight,
That shot across the deck;
And the binnacle pale and steady,
And the dull glimpse of the dead-eye,
And the sparks in fiery eddy
That whirled from the chimney neck.
In our jovial floating prison
There was sleep from fore to mizzen,
And never a star had risen
The hazy sky to speck.

Strange company we harbored,
We'd a hundred Jews to larboard,
Unwashed, uncombed, unbarbered—
Jews black, and brown, and gray;
With terror it would seize ye,
And make your souls uneasy,
To see those Rabbis greasy,
Who did naught but scratch and pray:
Their dirty children puking—
Their dirty saucepans cooking—
Their dirty fingers hooking
Their swarming fleas away.

To starboard, Turks and Greeks were—

Whiskered and brown their cheeks were—
Enormous wide their breeks were,
Their pipes did puff alway;
Each on his mat allotted
In silence smoked and squatted,
Whilst round their children trotted
In pretty, pleasant play.
He can't but smile who traces
The smiles on those brown faces,
And the pretty, prattling graces
Of those small heathens gay.

And so the hours kept tolling,
And through the ocean rolling
Went the brave "Iberia" bowling
Before the break of day—

When A SQUALL, upon a sudden,
Came o'er the waters scudding;
And the clouds began to gather,
And the sea was lashed to lather,
And the lowering thunder grumbled,
And the lightning jumped and tumbled,
And the ship, and all the ocean,
Woke up in wild commotion.
Then the wind set up a howling,
And the poodle dog a yowling,
And the cocks began a crowing,
And the old cow raised a lowing,
As she heard the tempest blowing;
And fowls and geese did cackle,
And the cordage and the tackle
Began to shriek and crackle;
And the spray dashed o'er the funnels,
And down the deck in runnels;
And the rushing water soaks all,
From the seamen in the fo'ksal
To the stokers whose black faces
Peer out of their bed-places;
And the captain he was bawling,
And the sailors pulling, hauling,
And the quarter-deck tarpauling
Was shivered in the squalling;
And the passengers awaken,
Most pitifully shaken;
And the steward jumps up, and hastens
For the necessary basins.

Then the Greeks they groaned and quivered,
And they knelt, and moaned, and shivered,
As the plunging waters met them,
And splashed and overset them;
And they call in their emergence
Upon countless saints and virgins;
And their marrowbones are bended,
And they think the world is ended.

And the Turkish women for'ard
Were frightened and behorror'd;
And shrieking and bewildering,
The mothers clutched their children;
The men sung "Allah! Illah!
Mashallah Bismillah!"
As the warring waters doused them
And splashed them and soused them,
And they called upon the Prophet,
And thought but little of it.

Then all the fleas in Jewry
Jumped up and bit like fury;
And the progeny of Jacob
Did on the main-deck wake up
(I wot those greasy Rabbins
Would never pay for cabins);
And each man moaned and jabbered in
His filthy Jewish gaberdine,
In woe and lamentation,
And howling consternation.
And the splashing water drenches
Their dirty brats and wenches;
And they crawl from bales and benches
In a hundred thousand stenches.

This was the White Squall famous,
Which latterly o'ercame us,
And which all will well remember
On the 28th September;
When a Prussian captain of Lancers
(Those tight-laced, whiskered prancers)
Came on the deck astonished,
By that wild squall admonished,
And wondering cried, "Potztausend,
Wie ist der Stürm jetzt brausend?"
And looked at Captain Lewis,
Who calmly stood and blew his
Cigar in all the hustle,

And scorned the tempest's tussle,
And oft we've thought thereafter
How he beat the storm to laughter;
For well he knew his vessel
With that vain wind could wrestle;
And when a wreck we thought her,
And doomed ourselves to slaughter,
How gayly he fought her,
And through the hubbub brought her,
And as the tempest caught her,
Cried, "GEORGE! SOME BRANDY-AND-WATER!"

And when, its force expended,
The harmless storm was ended,
And as the sunrise splendid
Came blushing o'er the sea;
I thought, as day was breaking,
My little girls were waking,
And smiling, and making
A prayer at home for me.

1844.

Riding from Coleraine
(Famed for lovely Kitty),
Came a Cockney bound
Unto Derry city;
Weary was his soul,
Shivering and sad, he
Bumped along the road
Leads to Limavaddy.

Mountains stretch'd around,
Gloomy was their tinting,
And the horse's hoofs
Made a dismal clinting;
Wind upon the heath
Howling was and piping,
On the heath and bog,
Black with many a snipe in.
Mid the bogs of black,
Silver pools were flashing,
Crows upon their sides
Picking were and splashing.

Cockney on the car
Closer folds his plaidy,
Grumbling at the road
Leads to Limavaddy.

Through the crashing woods
Autumn brawld and bluster'd,
Tossing round about
Leaves the hue of mustard
Yonder lay Lough Foyle,
Which a storm was whipping,
Covering with mist
Lake, and shores and shipping.
Up and down the hill
(Nothing could be bolder),
Horse went with a raw
Bleeding on his shoulder.
"Where are horses changed?"
Said I to the laddy
Driving on the box:
"Sir, at Limavaddy."

Limavaddy inn's
But a humble bait-house,
Where you may procure
Whiskey and potatoes;
Landlord at the door
Gives a smiling welcome—
To the shivering wights
Who to his hotel come.

Landlady within
Sits and knits a stocking,
With a wary foot
Baby's cradle rocking.
To the chimney nook
Having, found admittance,
There I watch a pup
Playing with two kittens;
(Playing round the fire),
Which of blazing turf is,
Roaring to the pot
Which bubbles with the murphies.
And the cradled babe
Fond the mother nursed it,
Singing it a song
As she twists the worsted!

Up and down the stair
Two more young ones patter
(Twins were never seen
Dirtier nor fatter).
Both have mottled legs,
Both have snubby noses,
Both have— Here the host
Kindly interposes:
"Sure you must be froze
With the sleet and hail, sir:
So will you have some punch,
Or will you have some ale, sir?"

Presently a maid
Enters with the liquor
(Half a pint of ale
Frothing in a beaker).
Gads! didn't know
What my beating heart meant:
Hebe's self I thought
Entered the apartment.
As she came she smiled,
And the smile bewitching,
On my word and honor,
Lighted all the kitchen!

With a curtsy neat
Greeting the new comer,
Lovely, smiling Peg
Offers me the rummer;
But my trembling hand
Up the beaker tilted,
And the glass of ale
Every drop I spilt it:
Spilt it every drop
(Dames, who read my volumes,
Pardon such a word)
On my what-d'ye-call-'ems!

Witnessing the sight
Of that dire disaster,
Out began to laugh
Missis, maid, and master;
Such a merry peal
'Specially Miss Peg's was,
(As the glass of ale
Trickling down my legs was,)
That the joyful sound

Of that mingling laughter
Echoed in my ears
Many a long day after.

Such a silver peal!
In the meadows listening,
You who've heard the bells
Ringing to a christening;
You who ever heard
Caradori pretty,
Smiling like an angel,
Singing "Giovinetti;"
Fancy Peggy's laugh,
Sweet, and clear, and cheerful,
At my pantaloons
With half a pint of beer full!

When the laugh was done,
Peg, the pretty hussy,
Moved about the room
Wonderfully busy;
Now she looks to see
If the kettle keep hot;
Now she rubs the spoons,
Now she cleans the teapot;
Now she sets the cups
Trimly and secure:
Now she scours a pot,
And so it was I drew her.

Thus it was I drew her
Scouring of a kettle,
(Faith! her blushing cheeks
Redden'd on the metal!)
Ah! but 'tis in vain
That I try to sketch it;
The pot perhaps is like,
But Peggy's face is wretched.
No the best of lead
And of indian-rubber
Never could depict
That sweet kettle-scrubber!

See her as she moves
Scarce the ground she touches,
Airy as a fay,
Graceful as a duchess;
Bare her rounded arm,

Bare her little leg is,
Vestris never show'd
Ankles like to Peggy's.
Braided is her hair,
Soft her look and modest,
Slim her little waist
Comfortably bodiced.

This I do declare,
Happy is the laddy
Who the heart can share
Of Peg of Limavaddy.
Married if she were
Blest would be the daddy
Of the children fair
Of Peg of Limavaddy.
Beauty is not rare
In the land of Paddy,
Fair beyond compare
Is Peg of Limavaddy.

Citizen or Squire,
Tory, Whig, or Radi-
cal would all desire
Peg of Limavaddy.
Had I Homer's fire,
Or that of Serjeant Taddy,
Meetly I'd admire
Peg of Limavaddy.
And till I expire,
Or till I grow mad I
Will sing unto my lyre
Peg of Limavaddy!

MAY-DAY ODE

But yesterday a naked sod
The dandies sneered from Rotten Row,
And cantered o'er it to and fro:
And see 'tis done!
As though 'twere by a wizard's rod
A blazing arch of lucid glass
Leaps like a fountain from the grass
To meet the sun!

A quiet green but few days since,

With cattle browsing in the shade:
And here are lines of bright arcade
In order raised!
A palace as for fairy Prince,
A rare pavilion, such as man
Saw never since mankind began,
And built and glazed!

A peaceful place it was but now,
And lo! within its shining streets
A multitude of nations meets;
A countless throng
I see beneath the crystal bow,
And Gaul and German, Russ and Turk,
Each with his native handiwork
And busy tongue.

I felt a thrill of love and awe
To mark the different garb of each,
The changing tongue, the various speech
Together blent:
A thrill, methinks, like His who saw
"All people dwelling upon earth
Praising our God with solemn mirth
And one consent."

High Sovereign, in your Royal state,
Captains, and chiefs, and councillors,
Before the lofty palace doors
Are open set,—
Hush ere you pass the shining gate:
Hush! ere the heaving curtain draws,
And let the Royal pageant pause
A moment yet.

People and prince a silence keep!
Bow coronet and kingly crown.
Helmet and plume, bow lowly down,
The while the priest,
Before the splendid portal step,
(While still the wondrous banquet stays,)
From Heaven supreme a blessing prays
Upon the feast.

Then onwards let the triumph march;
Then let the loud artillery roll,
And trumpets ring, and joy-bells toll,
And pass the gate.

Pass underneath the shining arch,
'Neath which the leafy elms are green;
Ascend unto your throne, O Queen!
And take your state.

Behold her in her Royal place;
A gentle lady; and the hand
That sways the sceptre of this land,
How frail and weak!
Soft is the voice, and fair the face:
She breathes amen to prayer and hymn;
No wonder that her eyes are dim,
And pale her cheek.

This moment round her empire's shores
The winds of Austral winter sweep,
And thousands lie in midnight sleep
At rest to-day.
Oh! awful is that crown of yours,
Queen of innumerable realms
Sitting beneath the budding elms
Of English May!

A wondrous scepter 'tis to bear:
Strange mystery of God which set
Upon her brow yon coronet,—
The foremost crown
Of all the world, on one so fair!
That chose her to it from her birth,
And bade the sons of all the earth
To her bow down.

The representatives of man
Here from the far Antipodes,
And from the subject Indian seas,
In Congress meet;
From Afric and from Hindustan,
From Western continent and isle,
The envoys of her empire pile
Gifts at her feet;

Our brethren cross the Atlantic tides,
Loading the gallant decks which once
Roared a defiance to our guns,
With peaceful store;
Symbol of peace, their vessel rides!*
O'er English waves float Star and Stripe,
And firm their friendly anchors gripe

The father shore!

From Rhine and Danube, Rhone and Seine,
As rivers from their sources gush,
The swelling floods of nations rush,
And seaward pour:
From coast to coast in friendly chain,
With countless ships we bridge the straits,
And angry ocean separates
Europe no more.

From Mississippi and from Nile—
From Baltic, Ganges, Bosphorous,
In England's ark assembled thus
Are friend and guest.
Look down the mighty sunlit aisle,
And see the sumptuous banquet set,
The brotherhood of nations met.
Around the feast!

Along the dazzling colonnade,
Far as the straining eye can gaze,
Gleam cross and fountain, bell and vase,
In vistas bright;
And statues fair of nymph and maid,
And steeds and pards and Amazons,
Writhing and grappling in the bronze,
In endless fight.

To deck the glorious roof and dome,
To make the Queen a canopy,
The peaceful hosts of industry
Their standards bear.
Yon are the works of Brahmin loom;
On such a web of Persian thread
The desert Arab bows his head
And cries his prayer.

Look yonder where the engines toil:
These England's arms of conquest are,
The trophies of her bloodless war:
Brave weapons these.
Victorians over wave and soil,
With these she sails, she weaves, she tills,
Pierces the everlasting hills
And spans the seas.

The engine roars upon its race,

The shuttle whirs the woof,
The people hum from floor to roof,
With Babel tongue.
The fountain in the basin plays,
The chanting organ echoes clear,
An awful chorus 'tis to hear,
A wondrous song!

Swell, organ, swell your trumpet blast,
March, Queen and Royal pageant, march
By splendid aisle and springing arch
Of this fair Hall:
And see! above the fabric vast,
God's boundless Heaven is bending blue,
God's peaceful sunlight's beaming through,
And shines o'er all.

May, 1851.

* The U. S. frigate "St. Lawrence."

THE BALLAD OF BOUILLABAISSE

A street there is in Paris famous,
For which no rhyme our language yields,
Rue Neuve des Petits Champs its name is—
The New Street of the Little Fields.
And here's an inn, not rich and splendid,
But still in comfortable case;
The which in youth I oft attended,
To eat a bowl of Bouillabaisse.

This Bouillabaisse a noble dish is—
A sort of soup or broth, or brew,
Or hotchpotch of all sorts of fishes,
That Greenwich never could outdo;
Green herbs, red peppers, mussels, saffron,
Soles, onions, garlic, roach, and dace:
All these you eat at TERRÉ'S tavern,
In that one dish of Bouillabaisse.

Indeed, a rich and savory stew 'tis;
And true philosophers, methinks,
Who love all sorts of natural beauties,
Should love good victuals and good drinks.
And Cordelier or Benedictine

Might gladly, sure, his lot embrace,
Nor find a fast-day too afflicting,
Which served him up a Bouillabaisse.

I wonder if the house still there is?
Yes, here the lamp is, as before;
The smiling red-checked écaillère is
Still opening oysters at the door.
Is TERRÉ still alive and able?
I recollect his droll grimace:
He'd come and smile before your table,
And hope you liked your Bouillabaisse.

We enter—nothing's changed or older.
"How's Monsieur TERRÉ, waiter, pray?"
The waiter stares and shrugs his shoulder—
"Monsieur is dead this many a day."
"It is the lot of saint and sinner,
So honest TERRÉ'S run his race."
"What will Monsieur require for dinner?"
"Say, do you still cook Bouillabaisse?"

"Oh, oui, Monsieur," 's the waiter's answer;
"Quel vin Monsieur desire-t-il?"
"Tell me a good one."—"That I can, Sir:
The Chambertin with yellow seal."
"So TERRÉ'S gone," I say, and sink in
My old accustom'd corner-place,
"He's done with feasting and with drinking,
With Burgundy and Bouillabaisse."

My old accustom'd corner here is,
The table still is in the nook;
Ah! vanish'd many a busy year is
This well-known chair since last I took.
When first I saw ye, cari luoghi,
I'd scarce a beard upon my face,
And now a grizzled, grim old fogy,
I sit and wait for Bouillabaisse.

Where are you, old companions trusty
Of early days here met to dine?
Come, waiter! quick, a flagon crusty—
I'll pledge them in the good old wine.
The kind old voices and old faces
My memory can quick retrace;
Around the board they take their places,
And share the wine and Bouillabaisse.

There's JACK has made a wondrous marriage;
There's laughing TOM is laughing yet;
There's brave AUGUSTUS drives his carriage;
There's poor old FRED in the Gazette;
On JAMES'S head the grass is growing;
Good Lord! the world has wagged apace
Since here we set the Claret flowing,
And drank, and ate the Bouillabaisse.

Ah me! how quick the days are flitting!
I mind me of a time that's gone,
When here I'd sit, as now I'm sitting,
In this same place—but not alone.
A fair young form was nestled near me,
A dear, dear face looked fondly up,
And sweetly spoke and smiled to cheer me
—There's no one now to share my cup.

I drink it as the Fates ordain it.
Come, fill it, and have done with rhymes:
Fill up the lonely glass, and drain it
In memory of dear old times.
Welcome the wine, whate'er the seal is;
And sit you down and say your grace
With thankful heart, whate'er the meal is.
—Here comes the smoking Bouillabaisse!

THE MAHOGANY TREE

Christmas is here:
Winds whistle shrill,
Icy and chill,
Little care we:
Little we fear
Weather without,
Sheltered about
The Mahogany Tree.

Once on the boughs
Birds of rare plume
Sang, in its bloom;
Night-birds are we:
Here we carouse,
Singing like them,
Perched round the stem

Of the jolly old tree.

Here let us sport,
Boys, as we sit;
Laughter and wit
Flashing so free.
Life is but short—
When we are gone,
Let them sing on,
Round the old tree.

Evenings we knew,
Happy as this;
Faces we miss,
Pleasant to see.
Kind hearts and true,
Gentle and just,
Peace to your dust!
We sing round the tree.

Care, like a dun,
Lurks at the gate:
Let the dog wait;
Happy we'll be!
Drink, every one;
Pile up the coals,
Fill the red bowls,
Round the old tree!

Drain we the cup.—
Friend, art afraid?
Spirits are laid
In the Red Sea.
Mantle it up;
Empty it yet;
Let us forget,
Round the old tree.

Sorrows, begone!
Life and its ills,
Duns and their bills,
Bid we to flee.
Come with the dawn,
Blue-devil sprite,
Leave us to-night,
Round the old tree.

"A surgeon of the United States' army says that on inquiring of the Captain of his company, he found that NINE-TENTHS of the men had enlisted on account of some female difficulty."—Morning Paper.

Ye Yankee Volunteers!
It makes my bosom bleed
When I your story read,
Though oft 'tis told one.
So—in both hemispheres
The women are untrue,
And cruel in the New,
As in the Old one!

What—in this company
Of sixty sons of Mars,
Who march 'neath Stripes and Stars,
With fife and horn,
Nine-tenths of all we see
Along the warlike line
Had but one cause to join
This Hope Forlorn?

Deserters from the realm
Where tyrant Venus reigns,
You slipp'd her wicked chains,
Fled and out-ran her.
And now, with sword and helm,
Together banded are
Beneath the Stripe and Star
Embroider'd banner!

And is it so with all
The warriors ranged in line,
With lace bedizen'd fine
And swords gold-hilted—
Yon lusty corporal,
Yon color-man who gripes
The flag of Stars and Stripes—
Has each been jilted?

Come, each man of this line,
The privates strong and tall,
"The pioneers and all,"
The fifer nimble—
Lieutenant and Ensign,
Captain with epaulets,

And Blacky there, who beats
The clanging cymbal—

O cymbal-beating black,
Tell us, as thou canst feel,
Was it some Lucy Neal
Who caused thy ruin?
O nimble fifing Jack,
And drummer making din
So deftly on the skin,
With thy rat-tattooing—

Confess, ye volunteers,
Lieutenant and Ensign,
And Captain of the line,
As bold as Roman—
Confess, ye grenadiers,
However strong and tall,
The Conqueror of you all
Is Woman, Woman!

No corselet is so proof
But through it from her bow
The shafts that she can throw
Will pierce and rankle.
No champion e'er so tough,
But's in the struggle thrown,
And tripp'd and trodden down
By her slim ankle.

Thus always it was ruled:
And when a woman smiled,
The strong man was a child,
The sage a noodle.
Alcides was befool'd,
And silly Samson shorn,
Long, long ere you were horn,
Poor Yankee Doodle!

THE PEN AND THE ALBUM

"I am Miss Catherine's book," the album speaks;
"I've lain among your tomes these many weeks;
I'm tired of their old coats and yellow cheeks.

"Quick, Pen! and write a line with a good grace:

Come! draw me off a funny little face;
And, prithee, send me back to Chesham Place."

PEN
"I am my master's faithful old Gold Pen;
I've served him three long years, and drawn since then
Thousands of funny women and droll men.

"O Album! could I tell you all his ways
And thoughts, since I am his, these thousand days,
Lord, how your pretty pages I'd amaze!"

ALBUM
"His ways? his thoughts? Just whisper me a few;
Tell me a curious anecdote or two,
And write 'em quickly off, good Mordan, do!"

PEN
"Since he my faithful service did engage
To follow him through his queer pilgrimage,
I've drawn and written many a line and page.

"Caricatures I scribbled have, and rhymes,
And dinner-cards, and picture pantomimes;
And merry little children's books at times.

"I've writ the foolish fancy of his brain;
The aimless jest that, striking, hath caused pain;
The idle word that he'd wish back again.

"I've help'd him to pen many a line for bread;
To joke with sorrow aching in his head;
And make your laughter when his own heart bled.

"I've spoke with men of all degree and sort—
Peers of the land, and ladies of the Court;
Oh, but I've chronicled a deal of sport!

"Feasts that were ate a thousand days ago,
Biddings to wine that long hath ceased to flow,
Gay meetings with good fellows long laid low;

"Summons to bridal, banquet, burial, ball,
Tradesman's polite reminders of his small
Account due Christmas last—I've answered all.

"Poor Diddler's tenth petition for a half-
Guinea; Miss Bunyan's for an autograph;

So I refuse, accept, lament, or laugh,

"Condole, congratulate, invite, praise, scoff.
Day after day still dipping in my trough,
And scribbling pages after pages off.

"Day after day the labor's to be done,
And sure as comes the postman and the sun,
The indefatigable ink must run.

"Go back, my pretty little gilded tome,
To a fair mistress and a pleasant home,
Where soft hearts greet us whensoe'er we come!

"Dear, friendly eyes, with constant kindness lit,
However rude my verse, or poor my wit,
Or sad or gay my mood, you welcome it.

"Kind lady! till my last of lines is penn'd,
My master's love, grief, laughter, at an end,
Whene'er I write your name, may I write friend!

"Not all are so that were so in past years;
Voices, familiar once, no more he hears;
Names, often writ, are blotted out in tears.

"So be it:—joys will end and tears will dry—
Album! my master bids me wish good-by,
He'll send you to your mistress presently.

"And thus with thankful heart he closes you;
Blessing the happy hour when a friend he knew
So gentle, and so generous, and so true.

"Nor pass the words as idle phrases by;
Stranger! I never writ a flattery,
Nor sign'd the page that register'd a lie."

MRS. KATHERINE'S LANTERN

WRITTEN IN A LADY'S ALBUM

"Coming from a gloomy court,
Place of Israelite resort,
This old lamp I've brought with me.

Madam, on its panes you'll see
The initials K and E."

"An old lantern brought to me?
Ugly, dingy, battered, black!"
(Here a lady I suppose
Turning up a pretty nose)—
"Pray, sir, take the old thing back.
I've no taste for bricabrac."

"Please to mark the letters twain—"
(I'm supposed to speak again)—
"Graven on the lantern pane.
Can you tell me who was she,
Mistress of the flowery wreath,
And the anagram beneath—
The mysterious K E?

"Full a hundred years are gone
Since the little beacon shone
From a Venice balcony:
There, on summer nights, it hung,
And her Lovers came and sung
To their beautiful K E.

"Hush! in the canal below
Don't you hear the plash of oars
Underneath the lantern's glow,
And a thrilling voice begins
To the sound of mandolins?
Begins singing of amore
And delire and dolore—
O the ravishing tenore!

"Lady, do you know the tune?
Ah, we all of us have hummed it!
I've an old guitar has thrummed it,
Under many a changing moon.
Shall I try it? Do Re MI . .
What is this? Ma foi, the fact is,
That my hand is out of practice,
And my poor old fiddle cracked is,
And a man—I let the truth out,—
Who's had almost every tooth out,
Cannot sing as once he sung,
When he was young as you are young,
When he was young and lutes were strung,
And love-lamps in the casement hung."

LUCY'S BIRTHDAY

Seventeen rosebuds in a ring,
Thick with sister flowers beset,
In a fragrant coronet,
Lucy's servants this day bring.
Be it the birthday wreath she wears
Fresh and fair, and symbolling
The young number of her years,
The sweet blushes of her spring.

Types of youth and love and hope!
Friendly hearts your mistress greet,
Be you ever fair and sweet,
And grow lovelier as you ope!
Gentle nursling, fenced about
With fond care, and guarded so,
Scarce you've heard of storms without,
Frosts that bite or winds that blow!

Kindly has your life begun,
And we pray that heaven may send
To our floweret a warm sun,
A calm summer, a sweet end.
And where'er shall be her home,
May she decorate the place;
Still expanding into bloom,
And developing in grace.

THE CANE-BOTTOM'D CHAIR

In tattered old slippers that toast at the bars,
And a ragged old jacket perfumed with cigars,
Away from the world and its toils and its cares,
I've a snug little kingdom up four pair of stairs.

To mount to this realm is a toil, to be sure,
But the fire there is bright and the air rather pure;
And the view I behold on a sunshiny day
Is grand through the chimney-pots over the way.

This snug little chamber is cramm'd in all nooks
With worthless old knick-knacks and silly old books,

And foolish old odds and foolish old ends,
Crack'd bargains from brokers, cheap keepsakes from friends.

Old armor, prints, pictures, pipes, china, (all crack'd,)
Old rickety tables, and chairs broken-backed;
A twopenny treasury, wondrous to see;
What matter? 'tis pleasant to you, friend, and me.

No better divan need the Sultan require,
Than the creaking old sofa that basks by the fire;
And 'tis wonderful, surely, what music you get
From the rickety, ramshackle, wheezy spinet.

That praying-rug came from a Turcoman's camp;
By Tiber once twinkled that brazen old lamp;
A mameluke fierce yonder dagger has drawn:
'Tis a murderous knife to toast muffins upon.

Long, long through the hours, and the night, and the chimes,
Here we talk of old books, and old friends, and old times;
As we sit in a fog made of rich Latakie
This chamber is pleasant to you, friend, and me.

But of all the cheap treasures that garnish my nest,
There's one that I love and I cherish the best:
For the finest of couches that's padded with hair
I never would change thee, my cane-bottom'd chair.

'Tis a bandy-legg'd, high-shoulder'd, worm-eaten seat,
With a creaking old back, and twisted old feet;
But since the fair morning when Fanny sat there,
I bless thee and love thee, old cane-bottom'd chair.

If chairs have but feeling, in holding such charms,
A thrill must have pass'd through your wither'd old arms!
I look'd, and I long'd, and I wish'd in despair;
I wish'd myself turn'd to a cane-bottom'd chair.

It was but a moment she sat in this place,
She'd a scarf on her neck, and a smile on her face!
A smile on her face, and a rose in her hair,
And she sat there, and bloom'd in my cane-bottom'd chair.

And so I have valued my chair ever since,
Like the shrine of a saint, or the throne of a prince;
Saint Fanny, my patroness sweet I declare,
The queen of my heart and my cane-bottom'd chair.

When the candles burn low, and the company's gone,
In the silence of night as I sit here alone—
I sit here alone, but we yet are a pair—
My Fanny I see in my cane-bottom'd chair.

She comes from the past and revisits my room;
She looks as she then did, all beauty and bloom;
So smiling and tender, so fresh and so fair,
And yonder she sits in my cane-bottom'd chair.

LINES WRITTEN TO AN ALBUM PRINT

As on this pictured page I look,
This pretty tale of line and hook
As though it were a novel-book
Amuses and engages:
I know them both, the boy and girl;
She is the daughter of the Earl,
The lad (that has his hair in curl)
My lord the County's page has.

A pleasant place for such a pair!
The fields lie basking in the glare;
No breath of wind the heavy air
Of lazy summer quickens.
Hard by you see the castle tall;
The village nestles round the wall,
As round about the hen its small
Young progeny of chickens.

It is too hot to pace the keep;
To climb the turret is too steep;
My lord the earl is dozing deep,
His noonday dinner over:
The postern-warder is asleep
(Perhaps they've bribed him not to peep):
And so from out the gate they creep,
And cross the fields of clover.

Their lines into the brook they launch;
He lays his cloak upon a branch,
To guarantee his Lady Blanche
's delicate complexion:
He takes his rapier, from his haunch,

That beardless doughty champion staunch;
He'd drill it through the rival's paunch
That question'd his affection!

O heedless pair of sportsmen slack!
You never mark, though trout or jack,
Or little foolish stickleback,
Your baited snares may capture.
What care has SHE for line and hook?
She turns her back upon the brook,
Upon her lover's eyes to look
In sentimental rapture.

O loving pair! as thus I gaze
Upon the girl who smiles always,
The little hand that ever plays
Upon the lover's shoulder;
In looking at your pretty shapes,
A sort of envious wish escapes
(Such as the Fox had for the Grapes)
The Poet your beholder.

To be brave, handsome, twenty-two;
With nothing else on earth to do,
But all day long to bill and coo:
It were a pleasant calling.
And had I such a partner sweet;
A tender heart for mine to beat,
A gentle hand my clasp to meet;—
I'd let the world flow at my feet,
And never heed its brawling.

THE ROSE UPON MY BALCONY

The rose upon my balcony the morning air perfuming,
Was leafless all the winter time and pining for the spring;
You ask me why her breath is sweet, and why her cheek is blooming,
It is because the sun is out and birds begin to sing.

The nightingale, whose melody is through the greenwood ringing,
Was silent when the boughs were bare and winds were blowing keen:
And if, Mamma, you ask of me the reason of his singing,
It is because the sun is out and all the leaves are green.

Thus each performs his part, Mamma; the birds have found their voices,
The blowing rose a flush, Mamma, her bonny cheek to dye;

And there's sunshine in my heart, Mamma, which wakens and rejoices,
And so I sing and blush, Mamma, and that's the reason why.

"Quand vous serez bien vielle, le soir à la chandelle
Assise auprès du feu devisant et filant,
Direz, chantant mes vers en vous esmerveillant,
Ronsard m'a célébré du temps que j'étois belle."
Some winter night, shut snugly in
Beside the fagot in the hall,
I think I see you sit and spin,
Surrounded by your maidens all.
Old tales are told, old songs are sung,
Old days come back to memory;
You say, "When I was fair and young,
A poet sang of me!"

There's not a maiden in your hall,
Though tired and sleepy ever so,
But wakes, as you my name recall,
And longs the history to know.
And, as the piteous tale is said,
Of lady cold and lover true,
Each, musing, carries it to bed,
And sighs and envies you!

"Our lady's old and feeble now,"
They'll say; "she once was fresh and fair,
And yet she spurn'd her lover's vow,
And heartless left him to despair:
The lover lies in silent earth,
No kindly mate the lady cheers;
She sits beside a lonely hearth,
With threescore and ten years!"

Ah! dreary thoughts and dreams are those,
But wherefore yield me to despair,
While yet the poet's bosom glows,
While yet the dame is peerless fair!
Sweet lady mine! while yet 'tis time
Requite my passion and my truth,
And gather in their blushing prime
The roses of your youth!

AT THE CHURCH GATE

Although I enter not,
Yet round about the spot
Ofttimes I hover:
And near the sacred gate,
With longing eyes I wait,
Expectant of her.

The Minster bell tolls out
Above the city's rout,
And noise and humming:
They've hush'd the Minster bell:
The organ 'gins to swell:
She's coming, she's coming!

My lady comes at last,
Timid, and stepping fast,
And hastening hither,
With modest eyes downcast:
She comes—she's here—she's past—
May heaven go with her!

Kneel, undisturb'd, fair Saint!
Pour out your praise or plaint
Meekly and duly;
I will not enter there,
To sully your pure prayer
With thoughts unruly.

But suffer me to pace
Round the forbidden place,
Lingering a minute
Like outcast spirits who wait
And see through heaven's gate
Angels within it.

THE AGE OF WISDOM

Ho, pretty page, with the dimpled chin,
That never has known the Barber's shear,
All your wish is woman to win,
This is the way that boys begin,—
Wait till you come to Forty Year.

Curly gold locks cover foolish brains,
Billing and cooing is all your cheer;
Sighing and singing of midnight strains,
Under Bonnybell's window panes,—
Wait till you come to Forty Year.

Forty times over let Michaelmas pass,
Grizzling hair the brain doth clear—
Then you know a boy is an ass,
Then you know the worth of a lass,
Once you have come to Forty Year.

Pledge me round, I bid ye declare,
All good fellows whose beards are gray,
Did not the fairest of the fair
Common grow and wearisome ere
Ever a month was passed away?

The reddest lips that ever have kissed,
The brightest eyes that ever have shone,
May pray and whisper, and we not list,
Or look away, and never be missed,
Ere yet ever a month is gone.

Gillian's dead, God rest her bier,
How I loved her twenty years syne!
Marian's married, but I sit here
Alone and merry at Forty Year,
Dipping my nose in the Gascon wine.

SORROWS OF WERTHER

WERTHER had a love for Charlotte
Such as words could never utter;
Would you know how first he met her?
She was cutting bread and butter.

Charlotte was a married lady,
And a moral man was Werther,
And, for all the wealth of Indies,
Would do nothing for to hurt her.

So he sighed and pined and ogled,
And his passion boiled and bubbled,
Till he blew his silly brains out,
And no more was by it troubled.

Charlotte, having seen his body
Borne before her on a shutter,
Like a well-conducted person,
Went on cutting bread and butter.

A DOE IN THE CITY

Little KITTY LORIMER,
Fair, and young, and witty,
What has brought your ladyship
Rambling to the City?

All the Stags in Capel Court
Saw her lightly trip it;
All the lads of Stock Exchange
Twigg'd her muff and tippet.

With a sweet perplexity,
And a mystery pretty,
Threading through Threadneedle Street,
Trots the little KITTY.

What was my astonishment—
What was my compunction,
When she reached the Offices
Of the Didland Junction!

Up the Didland stairs she went,
To the Didland door, Sir;
Porters lost in wonderment,
Let her pass before, Sir.

"Madam," says the old chief Clerk,
"Sure we can't admit ye."
"Where's the Didland Junction deed?"
Dauntlessly says KITTY.

"If you doubt my honesty,
Look at my receipt, Sir."
Up then jumps the old chief Clerk,
Smiling as he meets her.

KITTY at the table sits
(Whither the old Clerk leads her),
"I deliver this," she says,

"As my act and deed, Sir."

When I heard these funny words
Come from lips so pretty;
This, I thought, should surely be
Subject for a ditty.

What! are ladies stagging it?
Sure, the more's the pity;
But I've lost my heart to her,—
Naughty little KITTY.

THE LAST OF MAY

(IN REPLY TO AN INVITATION DATED ON THE 1ST.)

By fate's benevolent award,
Should I survive the day,
I'll drink a bumper with my lord
Upon the last of May.

That I may reach that happy time
The kindly gods I pray,
For are not ducks and pease in prime
Upon the last of May?

At thirty boards, 'twixt now and then,
My knife and fork shall play;
But better wine and better men
I shall not meet in May.

And though, good friend, with whom I dine,
Your honest head is gray,
And, like this grizzled head of mine,
Has seen its last of May;

Yet, with a heart that's ever kind,
A gentle spirit gay,
You've spring perennial in your mind,
And round you make a May!

"AH, BLEAK AND BARREN WAS THE MOOR"

Ah! bleak and barren was the moor,

Ah! loud and piercing was the storm,
The cottage roof was shelter'd sure,
The cottage hearth was bright and warm—
An orphan-boy the lattice pass'd,
And, as he mark'd its cheerful glow,
Felt doubly keen the midnight blast,
And doubly cold the fallen snow.

They marked him as he onward press'd,
With fainting heart and weary limb;
Kind voices bade him turn and rest,
And gentle faces welcomed him.
The dawn is up—the guest is gone,
The cottage hearth is blazing still:
Heaven pity all poor wanderers lone!
Hark to the wind upon the hill!

SONG OF THE VIOLET

A humble flower long time I pined
Upon the solitary plain,
And trembled at the angry wind,
And shrunk before the bitter rain.
And oh! 'twas in a blessed hour
A passing wanderer chanced to see,
And, pitying the lonely flower,
To stoop and gather me.

I fear no more the tempest rude,
On dreary heath no more I pine,
But left my cheerless solitude,
To deck the breast of Caroline.
Alas our days are brief at best,
Nor long I fear will mine endure,
Though shelter'd here upon a breast
So gentle and so pure.

It draws the fragrance from my leaves,
It robs me of my sweetest breath,
And every time it falls and heaves,
It warns me of my coming death.
But one I know would glad forego
All joys of life to be as I;
An hour to rest on that sweet breast,
And then, contented, die!

Beside the old hall-fire—upon my nurse's knee,
Of happy fairy days—what tales were told to me!
I thought the world was once—all peopled with princesses,
And my heart would beat to hear—their loves and their distresses:
And many a quiet night,—in slumber sweet and deep,
The pretty fairy people—would visit me in sleep.

I saw them in my dreams—come flying east and west,
With wondrous fairy gifts—the newborn babe they bless'd;
One has brought a jewel—and one a crown of gold,
And one has brought a curse—but she is wrinkled and old.
The gentle queen turns pale—to hear those words of sin,
But the king he only laughs—and bids the dance begin.

The babe has grown to be—the fairest of the land,
And rides the forest green—a hawk upon her hand,
An ambling palfrey white—a golden robe and crown:
I've seen her in my dreams—riding up and down:
And heard the ogre laugh—as she fell into his snare,
At the little tender creature—who wept and tore her hair!

But ever when it seemed—her need was at the sorest,
A prince in shining mail—comes prancing through the forest,
A waving ostrich-plume—a buckler burnished bright;
I've seen him in my dreams—good sooth! a gallant knight.
His lips are coral red—beneath a dark moustache;
See how he waves his hand—and how his blue eyes flash!

"Come forth, thou Paynim knight!"—he shouts in accents clear.
The giant and the maid—both tremble his voice to hear.
Saint Mary guard him well!—he draws his falchion keen,
The giant and the knight—are fighting on the green.
I see them in my dreams—his blade gives stroke on stroke,
The giant pants and reels—and tumbles like an oak!

With what a blushing grace—he falls upon his knee
And takes the lady's hand—and whispers, "You are free!"
Ah! happy childish tales—of knight and faërie!
I waken from my dreams—but there's ne'er a knight for me;
I waken from my dreams—and wish that I could be
A child by the old hall-fire—upon my nurse's knee!

POCAHONTAS

Wearied arm and broken sword
Wage in vain the desperate fight:
Round him press a countless horde,
He is but a single knight.
Hark! a cry of triumph shrill
Through the wilderness resounds,
As, with twenty bleeding wounds,
Sinks the warrior, fighting still.

Now they heap the fatal pyre,
And the torch of death they light:
Ah! 'tis hard to die of fire!
Who will shield the captive knight?
Round the stake with fiendish cry
Wheel and dance the savage crowd,
Cold the victim's mien, and proud.
And his breast is bared to die.

Who will shield the fearless heart?
Who avert the murderous blade?
From the throng, with sudden start,
See there springs an Indian maid.
Quick she stands before the knight,
"Loose the chain, unbind the ring,
I am daughter of the king,
And I claim the Indian right!"

Dauntlessly aside she flings
Lifted axe and thirsty knife;
Fondly to his heart she clings,
And her bosom guards his life!
In the woods of Powhattan,
Still 'tis told by Indian fires,
How a daughter of their sires
Saved the captive Englishman.

FROM POCAHONTAS

Returning from the cruel fight
How pale and faint appears my knight!
He sees me anxious at his side;
"Why seek, my love, your wounds to hide?
Or deem your English girl afraid
To emulate the Indian maid?"

Be mine my husband's grief to cheer
In peril to be ever near;
Whate'er of ill or woe betide,
To bear it clinging at his side;
The poisoned stroke of fate to ward,
His bosom with my own to guard:
Ah! could it spare a pang to his,
It could not know a purer bliss!
'Twould gladden as it felt the smart,
And thank the hand that flung the dart!

LOVE-SONGS MADE EASY

WHAT MAKES MY HEART TO THRILL AND GLOW?

THE MAYFAIR LOVE-SONG

Winter and summer, night and morn,
I languish at this table dark;
My office window has a corn-
er looks into St. James's Park.
I hear the foot-guards' bugle-horn,
Their tramp upon parade I mark;
I am a gentleman forlorn,
I am a Foreign-Office Clerk.

My toils, my pleasures, every one,
I find are stale, and dull, and slow;
And yesterday, when work was done,
I felt myself so sad and low,
I could have seized a sentry's gun
My wearied brains out out to blow.
What is it makes my blood to run?
What makes my heart to beat and glow?

My notes of hand are burnt, perhaps?
Some one has paid my tailor's bill?
No: every morn the tailor raps;
My I O U's are extant still.
I still am prey of debt and dun;
My elder brother's stout and well.
What is it makes my blood to run?
What makes my heart to glow and swell?

I know my chief's distrust and hate;

He says I'm lazy, and I shirk.
Ah! had I genius like the late
Right Honorable Edmund Burke!
My chance of all promotion's gone,
I know it is,—he hates me so.
What is it makes my blood to run,
And all my heart to swell and glow?

Why, why is all so bright and gay?
There is no change, there is no cause;
My office-time I found to-day
Disgusting as it ever was.
At three, I went and tried the Clubs,
And yawned and saunter'd to and fro;
And now my heart jumps up and throbs,
And all my soul is in a glow.

At half-past four I had the cab;
I drove as hard as I could go.
The London sky was dirty drab,
And dirty brown the London snow.
And as I rattled in a cant-
er down by dear old Bolton Row,
A something made my heart to pant,
And caused my cheek to flush and glow.

What could it be that made me find
Old Jawkins pleasant at the Club?
Why was it that I laughed and grinned
At whist, although I lost the rub?
What was it made me drink like mad
Thirteen small glasses of Curaço?
That made my inmost heart so glad,
And every fibre thrill and glow?

She's home again! she's home, she's home!
Away all cares and griefs and pain;
I knew she would—she's back from Rome;
She's home again! she's home again!
"The family's gone abroad," they said,
September last they told me so;
Since then my lonely heart is dead,
My blood I think's forgot to flow.

She's home again! away all care!
O fairest form the world can show!
O beaming eyes! O golden hair!
O tender voice, that breathes so low!

O gentlest, softest, purest heart!
O joy, O hope!—"My tiger, ho!"
Fitz-Clarence said; we saw him start—
He galloped down to Bolton Row.

THE GHAZUL, OR ORIENTAL LOVE-SONG

THE ROCKS.
I was a timid little antelope;
My home was in the rocks, the lonely rocks.

I saw the hunters scouring on the plain;
I lived among the rocks, the lonely rocks.

I was a-thirsty in the summer-heat;
I ventured to the tents beneath the rocks.

Zuleikah brought me water from the well;
Since then I have been faithless to the rocks.

I saw her face reflected in the well;
Her camels since have marched into the rocks.

I look to see her image in the well;
I only see my eyes, my own sad eyes.
My mother is alone among the rocks.

THE MERRY BARD

Zuleikah! The young Agas in the bazaar are slim-wasted and wear yellow slippers. I am old and hideous. One of my eyes is out, and the hairs of my beard are mostly gray. Praise be to Allah! I am a merry bard.

There is a bird upon the terrace of the Emir's chief wife. Praise be to Allah! He has emeralds on his neck, and a ruby tail. I am a merry bard. He deafens me with his diabolical screaming.

There is a little brown bird in the basket-maker's cage. Praise be to Allah! He ravishes my soul in the moonlight. I am a merry bard.

The peacock is an Aga, but the little bird is a Bulbul.

I am a little brown Bulbul. Come and listen in the moonlight.

Praise be to Allah! I am a merry bard.

THE CAÏQUE

Yonder to the kiosk, beside the creek,
Paddle the swift caïque.
Thou brawny oarsman with the sunburnt cheek,
Quick! for it soothes my heart to hear the Bulbul speak.

Ferry me quickly to the Asian shores,
Swift bending to your oars.
Beneath the melancholy sycamores,
Hark! what a ravishing note the lovelorn Bulbul pours.

Behold, the boughs seem quivering with delight,
The stars themselves more bright,
As mid the waving branches out of sight
The Lover of the Rose sits singing through the night.

Under the boughs I sat and listened still,
I could not have my fill.
"How comes," I said, "such music to his bill?
Tell me for whom he sings so beautiful a trill."

"Once I was dumb," then did the Bird disclose,
"But looked upon the Rose;
And in the garden where the loved one grows,
I straightway did begin sweet music to compose."

"O bird of song, there's one in this caïque
The Rose would also seek,
So he might learn like you to love and speak."
Then answered me the bird of dusky beak,
"The Rose, the Rose of Love blushes on Leilah's cheek."

MY NORA

Beneath the gold acacia buds
My gentle Nora sits and broods,
Far, far away in Boston woods
My gentle Nora!

I see the tear-drop in her e'e,
Her bosom's heaving tenderly;

I know—I know she thinks of me,
My Darling Nora!

And where am I? My love, whilst thou
Sitt'st sad beneath the acacia bough,
Where pearl's on neck, and wreath on brow,
I stand, my Nora!

Mid carcanet and coronet,
Where joy-lamps shine and flowers are set—
Where England's chivalry are met,
Behold me, Nora!

In this strange scene of revelry,
Amidst this gorgeous chivalry,
A form I saw was like to thee,
My love—my Nora!

She paused amidst her converse glad;
The lady saw that I was sad,
She pitied the poor lonely lad,—
Dost love her, Nora?

In sooth, she is a lovely dame,
A lip of red, and eye of flame,
And clustering golden locks, the same
As thine, dear Nora?

Her glance is softer than the dawn's,
Her foot is lighter than the fawn's,
Her breast is whiter than the swan's,
Or thine, my Nora!

Oh, gentle breast to pity me!
Oh, lovely Ladye Emily!
Till death—till death I'll think of thee—
Of thee and Nora!

TO MARY

I seem, in the midst of the crowd,
The lightest of all;
My laughter rings cheery and loud,
In banquet and ball.
My lip hath its smiles and its sneers,
For all men to see;

But my soul, and my truth, and my tears,
Are for thee, are for thee!

Around me they flatter and fawn—
The young and the old.
The fairest are ready to pawn
Their hearts for my gold.
They sue me—I laugh as I spurn
The slaves at my knee;
But in faith and in fondness I turn
Unto thee, unto thee!

SERENADE

Now the toils of day are over,
And the sun hath sunk to rest,
Seeking, like a fiery lover,
The bosom of the blushing west—

The faithful night keeps watch and ward,
Raising the moon her silver shield,
And summoning the stars to guard
The slumbers of my fair Mathilde!

The faithful night! Now all things lie
Hid by her mantle dark and dim,
In pious hope I hither hie,
And humbly chant mine ev'ning hymn.

Thou art my prayer, my saint, my shrine!
(For never holy pilgrim kneel'd,
Or wept at feet more pure than thine),
My virgin love, my sweet Mathilde!

THE MINARET BELLS

Tink-a-tink, tink-a-tink,
By the light of the star,
On the blue river's brink,
I heard a guitar.

I heard a guitar,
On the blue waters clear,
And knew by its music,

That Selim was near!

Tink-a-tink, tink-a-tink,
How the soft music swells,
And I hear the soft clink
Of the minaret bells!

COME TO THE GREENWOOD TREE

Come to the greenwood tree,
Come where the dark woods be,
Dearest, O come with me!
Let us rove—O my love—O my love!

Come—'tis the moonlight hour,
Dew is on leaf and flower,
Come to the linden bower,—
Let us rove—O my love—O my love!

Dark is the wood, and wide
Dangers, they say, betide;
But, at my Albert's side,
Nought I fear, O my love—O my love!

Welcome the greenwood tree,
Welcome the forest free,
Dearest, with thee, with thee,
Nought I fear, O my love—O my love!

FIVE GERMAN DITTIES

A TRAGIC STORY

BY ADELBERT VON CHAMISSO
"—'s war Einer, dem's zu Herzen gieng."

There lived a sage in days of yore
And he a handsome pigtail wore;
But wondered much and sorrowed more
Because it hung behind him.

He mused upon this curious case,
And swore he'd change the pigtail's place,
And have it hanging at his face,

Not dangling there behind him.

Says he, "The mystery I've found,—
I'll turn me round,"—he turned him round;
But still it hung behind him.

Then round, and round, and out and in,
All day the puzzled sage did spin;
In vain—it mattered not a pin,—
The pigtail hung behind him.

And right, and left, and round about,
And up, and down, and in, and out,
He turned; but still the pigtail stout
Hung steadily behind him.

And though his efforts never slack,
And though he twist, and twirl, and tack,
Alas! still faithful to his back
The pigtail hangs behind him.

THE CHAPLET

FROM UHLAND
"Es pflückte Blümlein mannigfalt."

A little girl through field and wood
Went plucking flowerets here and there,
When suddenly beside her stood
A lady wondrous fair!

The lovely lady smiled, and laid
A wreath upon the maiden's brow;
"Wear it, 'twill blossom soon," she said,
"Although 'tis leafless now."

The little maiden older grew
And wandered forth of moonlight eves,
And sighed and loved as maids will do;
When, lo! her wreath bore leaves.

Then was our maid a wife, and hung
Upon a joyful bridegroom's bosom;
When from the garland's leaves there sprung
Fair store of blossom.

And presently a baby fair
Upon her gentle breast she reared;
When midst the wreath that bound her hair
Rich golden fruit appeared.

But when her love lay cold in death,
Sunk in the black and silent tomb,
All sere and withered was the wreath
That wont so bright to bloom.

Yet still the withered wreath she wore;
She wore it at her dying hour;
When, to the wondrous garland bore
Both leaf, and fruit, and flower!

THE KING ON THE TOWER

FROM UHLAND
"Da liegen sie alle, die grauen Höhen."

The cold gray hills they bind me around,
The darksome valleys lie sleeping below,
But the winds as they pass o'er all this ground,
Bring me never a sound of woe!

Oh! for all I have suffered and striven,
Care has embittered my cup and my feast;
But here is the night and the dark blue heaven,
And my soul shall be at rest.

O golden legends writ in the skies!
I turn towards you with longing soul,
And list to the awful harmonies
Of the Spheres as on they roll.

My hair is gray and my sight nigh gone;
My sword it rusteth upon the wall;
Right have I spoken, and right have I done:
When shall I rest me once for all?

O blessed rest! O royal night!
Wherefore seemeth the time so long
Till I see you stars in their fullest light,
And list to their loudest song?

ON A VERY OLD WOMAN

LA MOTTE FOUQUÉ
"Und Du gingst einst, die Myrt' im Haare."

And thou wert once a maiden fair,
A blushing virgin warm and young:
With myrtles wreathed in golden hair,
And glossy brow that knew no care—
Upon a bridegroom's arm you hung.

The golden locks are silvered now,
The blushing cheek is pale and wan;
The spring may bloom, the autumn glow,
All's one—in chimney corner thou
Sitt'st shivering on.—

A moment—and thou sink'st to rest!
To wake perhaps an angel blest,
In the bright presence of thy Lord.
Oh, weary is life's path to all!
Hard is the strife, and light the fall,
But wondrous the reward!

A CREDO

I
For the sole edification
Of this decent congregation,
Goodly people, by your grant
I will sing a holy chant—
I will sing a holy chant.
If the ditty sound but oddly,
'Twas a father, wise and godly,
Sang it so long ago—
Then sing as Martin Luther sang,
As Doctor Martin Luther sang:
"Who loves not wine, woman and song,
He is a fool his whole life long!"

II
He, by custom patriarchal,
Loved to see the beaker sparkle;
And he thought the wine improved,

Tasted by the lips he loved—
By the kindly lips he loved.
Friends, I wish this custom pious
Duly were observed by us,
To combine love, song, wine,
And sing as Martin Luther sang,
As Doctor Martin Luther sang:
"Who loves not wine, woman and song,
He is a fool his whole life long!"

III
Who refuses this our Credo,
And who will not sing as we do,
Were he holy as John Knox,
I'd pronounce him heterodox!
I'd pronounce him heterodox,
And from out this congregation,
With a solemn commination,
Banish quick the heretic,
Who will not sing as Luther sang,
As Doctor Martin Luther sang:
"Who loves not wine, woman and song,
He is a fool his whole life long!"

FOUR IMITATIONS OF BÉRANGER

LE ROI D'YVETOT

Il était un roi d'Yvetot,
Peu connu dans l'histoire;
Se levant tard, se couchant tôt,
Dormant fort bien sans gloire,
Et couronné par Jeanneton
D'un simple bonnet de coton,
Dit-on.
Oh! oh! oh! oh! ah! ah! ah! ah!
Quel bon petit roi c'était la!
La, la.

Il fesait ses quatre repas
Dans son palais de chaume,
Et sur un âne, pas à pas,
Parcourait son royaume.
Joyeux, simple et croyant le bien,
Pour toute garde il n'avait rien
Qu'un chien.

Oh! oh! oh ! oh! ah! ah! ah! ah! &c.

Il n'avait de goût onéreux
Qu'une soif un peu vive;
Mais, en rendant son peuple heureux,
Il faut bien qu'un roi vive.
Lui-même à table, et sans suppôt,
Sur chaque muid levait un pot
D'impôt.
Oh! oh! oh! oh! ah! ah! ah! ah! &c.

Aux filles de bonnes maisons
Comme il avait su plaire,
Ses sujets avaient cent raisons
De le nommer leur père:
D'ailleurs il ne levait de ban
Que pour tirer quatre fois l'an
Au blanc.
Oh! oh! oh! oh! ah! ah! ah! ah! &c.

Il n'agrandit point ses états,
Fut un voisin commode,
Et, modèle des potentats,
Prit le plaisir pour code.
Ce n'est que loraqu'il expira,
Que le peuple qui l'enterra
Pleura.
Oh! oh! oh! oh! ah! ah! ah! ah! &c.

On conserve encor le portrait
De ce digne et bon prince;
C'est l'enseigne d'un cabaret
Fameux dans la province.
Les jours de fête, bien souvent,
La foule s'écrie en buvant
Devant:
Oh! oh! oh! oh! ah! ah! ah! ah! &c.

THE KING OF YVETOT

There was a king of Yvetot,
Of whom renown hath little said,
Who let all thoughts of glory go,
And dawdled half his days a-bed;
And every night, as night came round,
By Jenny, with a nightcap crowned,

Slept very sound:
Sing ho, ho, ho! and he, he, he!
That's the kind of king for me.

And every day it came to pass,
That four lusty meals made he;
And, step by step, upon an ass,
Rode abroad, his realms to see;
And wherever he did stir,
What think you was his escort, sir?
Why, an old cur.
Sing ho, ho, ho ! &c.

If e'er he went into excess,
'Twas from a somewhat lively thirst;
But he who would his subjects bless,
Odd's fish!—must wet his whistle first;
And so from every cask they got,
Our king did to himself allot,
At least a pot.
Sing ho, ho! &c.

To all the ladies of the land,
A courteous king, and kind, was he;
The reason why you'll understand,
They named him Pater Patriae.
Each year he called his fighting men,
And marched a league from home, and then
Marched back again.
Sing ho, ho! &c.

Neither by force nor false pretence,
He sought to make his kingdom great,
And made (O princes, learn from hence),—
"Live and let live," his rule of state.
'Twas only when he came to die,
That his people who stood by,
Were known to cry.
Sing ho, ho! &c.

The portrait of this best of kings
Is extant still, upon a sign
That on a village tavern swings,
Famed in the country for good wine.
The people in their Sunday trim,
Filling their glasses to the brim,
Look up to him,
Singing ha, ha, ha! and he, he, he!

That's the sort of king for me.

THE KING OF BRENTFORD.

ANOTHER VERSION

There was a king in Brentford,—of whom no legends tell,
But who, without his glory,—could eat and sleep right well.
His Polly's cotton nightcap,—it was his crown of state,
He slept of evenings early,—and rose of mornings late.

All in a fine mud palace,—each day he took four meals,
And for a guard of honor,—a dog ran at his heels,
Sometimes, to view his kingdoms,—rode forth this monarch good,
And then a prancing jackass—he royally bestrode.

There were no costly habits—with which this king was curst,
Except (and where's the harm on't?)—a somewhat lively thirst;
But people must pay taxes,—and kings must have their sport,
So out of every gallon—His Grace he took a quart.

He pleased the ladies round him,—with manners soft and bland;
With reason good, they named him,—the father of his land.
Each year his mighty armies—marched forth in gallant show;
Their enemies were targets—their bullets they were tow.

He vexed no quiet neighbor,—no useless conquest made,
But by the laws of pleasure,—his peaceful realm he swayed.
And in the years he reigned,—through all this country wide,
There was no cause for weeping,—save when the good man died.

The faithful men of Brentford,—do still their king deplore,
His portrait yet is swinging,—beside an alehouse door.
And topers, tender-hearted,—regard his honest phiz,
And envy times departed—that knew a reign like his.

LE GRENIER

Je viens revoir l'asile où ma jeunesse
De la misère a subi les leçons.
J'avais vingt ans, une folle maîtresse,
De francs amis et l'amour des chansons.
Bravant le monde et les sots et les sages,
Sans avenir, riche de mon printemps,

Leste et joyeux je montais six étages,
Dans un grenier qu'on est bien a vingt ans.

C'est un grenier, point ne veux qu'on l'ignore.
Là fut mon lit, bien chétif et bien dur;
Là fut ma table; et je retrouve encore
Trois pieds d'un vers charbonnés sur le mur.
Apparaissez, plaisirs de mon bel âge,
Que d'un coup d'aile a fustigés le temps,
Vingt fois pour vous j'ai ma montre en gage.
Dans un grenier qu'on est bien à vingt ans!

Lisette ici doit surtout apparaître,
Vive, jolie, avec un frais chapeau;
Déjà sa main à l'étroite fenêtre
Suspend son schal, en guise de rideau.
Sa robe aussi va parer ma couchette;
Respecte, Amour, ses plis longs et flottans.
Jai su depuis qui payait sa toilette
Dans un grenier qu'on est bien à vingt ans!

A table un jour, jour de grande richesse,
De mes amis les voix brillaient en choeur,
Quand jusqu'ici monte on cri d'allégresse;
A Marengo Bonaparte est vainqueur.
Le canon gronde; un autre chant commence;
Nous célébrons tant de faits éclatans.
Les rois jamais n'envahiront la France.
Dans un grenier qu'on est bien à vingt ans!

Quittons ce toit où ma raison s'enivre.
Oh! qu'ils sont loin ces jours si regrettés!
J'echangerais ce qu'il me reste à vivre
Contre un des mois qu'ici Dieu ma comptés.
Pour rêver gloire, amour, plaisir, folie,
Pour dépenser sa vie en peu d'instans,
D'un long espoir pour la voir embellie,
Dans un grenier qu'on est bien à vingt ans!

THE GARRET

With pensive eyes the little room I view,
Where, in my youth, I weathered it so long;
With a wild mistress, a stanch friend or two,
And a light heart still breaking into song:
Making a mock of life, and all its cares,

Rich in the glory of my rising sun,
Lightly I vaulted up four pair of stairs,
In the brave days when I was twenty-one.

Yes; 'tis a garret—let him know't who will—
There was my bed—full hard it was and small;
My table there—and I decipher still
Half a lame couplet charcoaled on the wall.
Ye joys, that Time hath swept with him away,
Come to mine eyes, ye dreams of love and fun;
For you I pawned my watch how many a day,
In the brave days when I was twenty-one.

And see my little Jessy, first of all;
She comes with pouting lips and sparkling eyes:
Behold, how roguishly she pins her shawl
Across the narrow casement, curtain-wise;
Now by the bed her petticoat glides down,
And when did woman look the worse in none?
I have heard since who paid for many a gown,
In the brave days when I was twenty-one.

One jolly evening, when my friends and I
Made happy music with our songs and cheers,
A shout of triumph mounted up thus high,
And distant cannon opened on our ears:
We rise,—we join in the triumphant strain,—
Napoleon conquers—Austerlitz is won—
Tyrants shall never tread us down again,
In the brave days when I was twenty-one.

Let us begone—the place is sad and strange—
How far, far off, these happy times appear;
All that I have to live I'd gladly change
For one such month as I have wasted here—
To draw long dreams of beauty, love, and power,
From founts of hope that never will outrun,
And drink all life's quintessence in an hour,
Give me the days when I was twenty-one!

ROGER-BONTEMPS

Aux gens atrabilaires
Pour exemple donné,
En un temps de misères
Roger-Bontemps est né.

Vivre obscur à sa guise,
Narguer les mécontens;
Eh gai! c'est la devise
Du gros Roger-Bontemps.

Du chapeau de son père
Coîffé dans les grands jours,
De roses ou de lierre
Le rajeunir toujours;
Mettre un manteau de bure,
Vieil ami de vingt ans;
Eh gai! c'est la parure
Du gros Roger-Bontemps.

Posséder dans en hutte
Une table, un vieux lit,
Des cartes, une flûte,
Un broc que Dieu remplit;
Un portrait de maîtresse,
Un coffre et rien dedans;
Eh gai! c'est la richesse
Du gros Roger-Bontemps.

Aux enfans de la ville
Montrer de petite jeux;
Etre fesseur habile
De contes graveleux;
Ne parler que de danse
Et d'almanachs chantans:
Eh gai! c'est la science
Du gros Roger-bontemps.

Faute de vins d'élite,
Sabler ceux du canton:
Préférer Marguerite
Aux dames du grand ton:
De joie et de tendresse
Remplir tous ses instans:
Eh gai! c'est la sagesse
Du gros Roger-Bontemps.

Dire au ciel: Je me fie,
Mon père, à ta bonté;
De ma philosophie
Pardonne le gaîté;
Que ma saison dernière
Soit encore un printemps;
Eh gai! c'est la prière

Du gros Roger-Bontemps.

Vous pauvres pleins d'envie,
Vous riches désireux,
Vous, dont le char dévie
Après un cours heureux;
Vous qui perdrez peut-être
Des titres éclatans,
Eh gai! prenez pour maître
Le gros Roger-Bontemps.

JOLLY JACK

When fierce political debate
Throughout the isle was storming,
And Rads attacked the throne and state,
And Tories the reforming,
To calm the furious rage of each,
And right the land demented,
Heaven sent us Jolly Jack, to teach
The way to be contented.

Jack's bed was straw, 'twas warm and soft,
His chair, a three-legged stool;
His broken jug was emptied oft,
Yet, somehow, always full.
His mistress' portrait decked the wall,
His mirror had a crack;
Yet, gay and glad, though this was all
His wealth, lived Jolly Jack.

To give advice to avarice,
Teach pride its mean condition,
And preach good sense to dull pretence,
Was honest Jack's high mission.
Our simple statesman found his rule
Of moral in the flagon,
And held his philosophic school
Beneath the "George and Dragon."

When village Solons cursed the Lords,
And called the malt-tax sinful,
Jack heeded not their angry words,
But smiled and drank his skinful.
And when men wasted health and life,
In search of rank and riches,

Jack marked aloof the paltry strife,
And wore his threadbare breeches.

"I enter not the church," he said,
"But I'll not seek to rob it;"
So worthy Jack Joe Miller read,
While others studied Cobbett.
His talk it was of feast and fun;
His guide the Almanack;
From youth to age thus gayly run
The life of Jolly Jack.

And when Jack prayed, as oft he would,
He humbly thanked his Maker;
"I am," said he, "O Father good!
Nor Catholic nor Quaker:
Give each his creed, let each proclaim
His catalogue of curses;
I trust in Thee, and not in them,
In Thee, and in Thy mercies!

"Forgive me if, midst all Thy works,
No hint I see of damning;
And think there's faith among the Turks,
And hope for e'en the Brahmin.
Harmless my mind is, and my mirth,
And kindly is my laughter:
I cannot see the smiling earth,
And think there's hell hereafter."

Jack died; he left no legacy,
Save that his story teaches:—
Content to peevish poverty;
Humility to riches.
Ye scornful great, ye envious small,
Come follow in his track;
We all were happier, if we all
Would copy JOLLY JACK.

IMITATION OF HORACE

TO HIS SERVING BOY

Persicos odi
Puer, apparatus;
Displicent nexae

Philyrâ coronae:
Mitte sectari,
Rosa qua locorum
Sera moretur.

Simplici myrto
Nihil allabores
Sedulus, curo:
Neque te ministrum
Dedecet myrtus,
Neque me sub arctâ
Vite bibentem.

AD MINISTRAM

Dear LUCY, you know what my wish is,—
I hate all your Frenchified fuss:
Your silly entrées and made dishes
Were never intended for us.
No footman in lace and in ruffles
Need dangle behind my arm-chair;
And never mind seeking for truffles,
Although they be ever so rare.

But a plain leg of mutton, my Lucy,
I prithee get ready at three:
Have it smoking, and tender and juicy,
And what better meat can there be?
And when it has feasted the master,
'Twill amply suffice for the maid;
Meanwhile I will smoke my canaster,
And tipple my ale in the shade.

OLD FRIENDS WITH NEW FACES

THE KNIGHTLY GUERDON*

Untrue to my Ulric I never could be,
I vow by the saints and the blessed Marie,
Since the desolate hour when we stood by the shore,
And your dark galley waited to carry you o'er:
My faith then I plighted, my love I confess'd,
As I gave you the BATTLE-AXE marked with your crest!

When the bold barons met in my father's old hall,
Was not Edith the flower of the banquet and ball?
In the festival hour, on the lips of your bride,
Was there ever a smile save with THEE at my side?
Alone in my turret I loved to sit best,
To blazon your BANNER and broider your crest.

The knights were assembled, the tourney was gay!
Sir Ulric rode first in the warrior-mêlée.
In the dire battle-hour, when the tourney was done,
And you gave to another the wreath you had won!
Though I never reproached thee, cold, cold was my breast,
As I thought of that BATTLE-AXE, ah! and that crest!

But away with remembrance, no more will I pine
That others usurped for a time what was mine!
There's a FESTIVAL HOUR for my Ulric and me:
Once more, as of old, shall he bend at my knee;
Once more by the side of the knight I love best
Shall I blazon his BANNER and broider his crest.

"Your Molly has never been false," she declares,
"Since the last time we parted at Wapping Old Stairs;
When I said that I would continue the same,
And I gave you the 'bacco-box marked with my name.
When I passed a whole fortnight between decks with you,
Did I e'er give a kiss, Tom, to one of your crew?
To be useful and kind to my Thomas I stay'd,
For his trousers I washed, and his grog too I made.

"Though you promised last Sunday to walk in the Mall
With Susan from Deptford and likewise with Sall,
In silence I stood your unkindness to hear
And only upbraided my Tom with a tear.
Why should Sall, or should Susan, than me be more prized?
For the heart that is true, Tom, should ne'er be despised;
Then be constant and kind, nor your Molly forsake,
Still your trousers I'll wash and your grog too I'll make."

* "WAPPING OLD STAIRS.

THE ALMACK'S ADIEU

Your Fanny was never false-hearted,
And this she protests and she vows,
From the triste moment when we parted

On the staircase of Devonshire House!
I blushed when you asked me to marry,
I vowed I would never forget;
And at parting I gave my dear Harry
A beautiful vinegarette!

We spent en province all December,
And I ne'er condescended to look
At Sir Charles, or the rich county member,
Or even at that darling old Duke.
You were busy with dogs and with horses,
Alone in my chamber I sat,
And made you the nicest of purses,
And the smartest black satin cravat!

At night with that vile Lady Frances
(Je faisois moi tapisserie)
You danced every one of the dances,
And never once thought of poor me!
Mon pauvre petit coeur! what a shiver
I felt as she danced the last set;
And you gave, O mon Dieu! to revive her
My beautiful vinegarette!

Return, love! away with coquetting;
This flirting disgraces a man!
And ah! all the while you're forgetting
The heart of your poor little Fan!
Reviens! break away from those Circes,
Reviens, for a nice little chat;
And I've made you the sweetest of purses,
And a lovely black satin cravat!

WHEN THE GLOOM IS ON THE GLEN

When the moonlight's on the mountain
And the gloom is on the glen,
At the cross beside the fountain
There is one will meet thee then.
At the cross beside the fountain;
Yes, the cross beside the fountain,
There is one will meet thee then!

I have braved, since first we met, love,
Many a danger in my course;
But I never can forget, love,

That dear fountain, that old cross,
Where, her mantle shrouded o'er her—
For the winds were chilly then—
First I met my Leonora,
When the gloom was on the glen.

Many a clime I've ranged since then, love,
Many a land I've wandered o'er;
But a valley like that glen, love,
Half so dear I never sor!
Ne'er saw maiden fairer, coyer,
Than wert thou, my true love, when
In the gloaming first I saw yer,
In the gloaming of the glen!

THE RED FLAG

Where the quivering lightning flings
His arrows from out the clouds,
And the howling tempest sings
And whistles among the shrouds,
'Tis pleasant, 'tis pleasant to ride
Along the foaming brine—
Wilt be the Rover's bride?
Wilt follow him, lady mine?
Hurrah!
For the bonny, bonny brine.

Amidst the storm and rack,
You shall see our galley pass,
As a serpent, lithe and black,
Glides through the waving grass.
As the vulture swift and dark,
Down on the ring-dove flies,
You shall see the Rovers bark
Swoop down upon his prize.
Hurrah!
For the bonny, bonny prize.

Over her sides we dash,
We gallop across her deck—
Ha! there's a ghastly gash
On the merchant-captain's neck—
Well shot, well shot, old Ned!
Well struck, well struck, black James!
Our arms are red, and our foes are dead,

And we leave a ship in flames!
Hurrah!
For the bonny, bonny flames!

DEAR JACK

Dear Jack, this white mug that with Guinness I fill,
And drink to the health of sweet Nan of the Hill,
Was once Tommy Tosspot's, as jovial a sot
As e'er drew a spigot, or drain'd a full pot—
In drinking all round 'twas his joy to surpass,
And with all merry tipplers he swigg'd off his glass.

One morning in summer, while seated so snug,
In the porch of his garden, discussing his jug,
Stern Death, on a sudden, to Tom did appear,
And said, "Honest Thomas, come take your last bier."
We kneaded his clay in the shape of this can,
From which let us drink to the health of my Nan.

COMMANDERS OF THE FAITHFUL

The Pope he is a happy man,
His Palace is the Vatican,
And there he sits and drains his can:
The Pope he is a happy man.
I often say when I'm at home,
I'd like to be the Pope of Rome.

And then there's Sultan Saladin,
That Turkish Soldan full of sin;
He has a hundred wives at least,
By which his pleasure is increased:
I've often wished, I hope no sin,
That I were Sultan Saladin.

But no, the Pope no wife may choose,
And so I would not wear his shoes;
No wine may drink the proud Paynim,
And so I'd rather not be him:
My wife, my wine, I love, I hope,
And would be neither Turk nor Pope.

WHEN MOONLIKE ORE THE HAZURE SEAS

When moonlike ore the hazure seas
In soft effulgence swells,
When silver jews and balmy breaze
Bend down the Lily's bells;
When calm and deap, the rosy sleep
Has lapt your soal in dreems,
R Hangeline! R lady mine!
Dost thou remember Jeames?

I mark thee in the Marble All,
Where England's loveliest shine—
I say the fairest of them hall
Is Lady Hangeline.
My soul, in desolate eclipse,
With recollection teems—
And then I hask, with weeping lips,
Dost thou remember Jeames?

Away! I may not tell thee hall
This soughring heart endures—
There is a lonely sperrit-call
That Sorrow never cures;
There is a little, little Star,
That still above me beams;
It is the Star of Hope—but ar!
Dost thou remember Jeames?

KING CANUTE

King Canute was weary hearted; he had reigned for years a score,
Battling, struggling, pushing, fighting, killing much and robbing more;
And he thought upon his actions, walking by the wild sea-shore.

'Twixt the Chancellor and Bishop walked the King with steps sedate,
Chamberlains and grooms came after, silversticks and goldsticks great,
Chaplains, aides-de-camp, and pages,—all the officers of state.

Sliding after like his shadow, pausing when he chose to pause,
If a frown his face contracted, straight the courtiers dropped their jaws;
If to laugh the king was minded, out they burst in loud hee-haws.

But that day a something vexed him, that was clear to old and young:
Thrice his Grace had yawned at table, when his favorite gleemen sung,

Once the Queen would have consoled him, but he bade her hold her tongue.

"Something ails my gracious master," cried the Keeper of the Seal.
"Sure, my lord, it is the lampreys served to dinner, or the veal?"
"Psha!" exclaimed the angry monarch, "Keeper, 'tis not that I feel.

"'Tis the HEART, and not the dinner, fool, that doth my rest impair:
Can a king be great as I am, prithee, and yet know no care?
Oh, I'm sick, and tired, and weary."—Some one cried, "The King's armchair!"

Then towards the lackeys turning, quick my Lord the Keeper nodded,
Straight the King's great chair was brought him, by two footmen able-bodied;
Languidly he sank into it: it was comfortably wadded.

"Leading on my fierce companions," cried he, "over storm and brine,
I have fought and I have conquered! Where was glory like to mine?"
Loudly all the courtiers echoed: "Where is glory like to thine?"

"What avail me all my kingdoms? Weary am I now and old;
Those fair sons I have begotten, long to see me dead and cold;
Would I were, and quiet buried, underneath the silent mould!

"Oh, remorse, the writhing serpent! at my bosom tears and bites;
Horrid, horrid things I look on, though I put out all the lights;
Ghosts of ghastly recollections troop about my bed at nights.

"Cities burning, convents blazing, red with sacrilegious fires;
Mothers weeping, virgins screaming vainly for their slaughtered sires.—"
"Such a tender conscience," cries the Bishop, "every one admires."

"But for such unpleasant bygones, cease, my gracious lord, to search,
They're forgotten and forgiven by our Holy Mother Church;
Never, never does she leave her benefactors in the lurch.

"Look! the land is crowned with minsters, which your Grace's bounty raised;
Abbeys filled with holy men, where you and Heaven are daily praised:
YOU, my lord, to think of dying? on my conscience I'm amazed!"

"Nay, I feel," replied King Canute, "that my end is drawing near."
"Don't say so," exclaimed the courtiers (striving each to squeeze a tear).
"Sure your Grace is strong and lusty, and may live this fifty year."

"Live these fifty years!" the Bishop roared, with actions made to suit.
"Are you mad, my good Lord Keeper, thus to speak of King Canute!
Men have lived a thousand years, and sure his Majesty will do't.

"Adam, Enoch, Lamech, Cainan, Mahaleel, Methusela,
Lived nine hundred years apiece, and mayn't the King as well as they?"

"Fervently," exclaimed the Keeper, "fervently I trust he may."

"HE to die?" resumed the Bishop. He a mortal like to US?
Death was not for him intended, though communis omnibus:
Keeper, you are irreligious, for to talk and cavil thus.

"With his wondrous skill in healing ne'er a doctor can compete,
Loathsome lepers, if he touch them, start up clean upon their feet;
Surely he could raise the dead up, did his Highness think it meet.

"Did not once the Jewish captain stay the sun upon the hill,
And, the while he slew the foemen, bid the silver moon stand still?
So, no doubt, could gracious Canute, if it were his sacred will."

"Might I stay the sun above us, good sir Bishop?" Canute cried;
"Could I bid the silver moon to pause upon her heavenly ride?
If the moon obeys my orders, sure I can command the tide.

"Will the advancing waves obey me, Bishop, if I make the sign?"
Said the Bishop, bowing lowly, "Land and sea, my lord, are thine."
Canute turned towards the ocean—"Back!" he said, "thou foaming brine.

"From the sacred shore I stand on, I command thee to retreat;
Venture not, thou stormy rebel, to approach thy master's seat:
Ocean, be thou still! I bid thee come not nearer to my feet!"

But the sullen ocean answered with a louder, deeper roar,
And the rapid waves drew nearer, falling sounding on the shore;
Back the Keeper and the Bishop, back the king and courtiers bore.

And he sternly bade them never more to kneel to human clay,
But alone to praise and worship That which earth and seas obey:
And his golden crown of empire never wore he from that day.
King Canute is dead and gone: Parasites exist alway.

FRIAR'S SONG

Some love the matin-chimes, which tell
The hour of prayer to sinner:
But better far's the mid-day bell,
Which speaks the hour of dinner;
For when I see a smoking fish,
Or capon drown'd in gravy,
Or noble haunch on silver dish,
Full glad I sing my ave.

My pulpit is an alehouse bench,
Whereon I sit so jolly;
A smiling rosy country wench
My saint and patron holy.
I kiss her cheek so red and sleek,
I press her ringlets wavy,
And in her willing ear I speak
A most religious ave.

And if I'm blind, yet heaven is kind,
And holy saints forgiving;
For sure he leads a right good life
Who thus admires good living.
Above, they say, our flesh is air,
Our blood celestial ichor:
Oh, grant! mid all the changes there,
They may not change our liquor!

ATRA CURA

Before I lost my five poor wits,
I mind me of a Romish clerk,
Who sang how Care, the phantom dark,
Beside the belted horseman sits.
Methought I saw the grisly sprite
Jump up but now behind my Knight.

And though he gallop as he may,
I mark that cursed monster black
Still sits behind his honor's back,
Tight squeezing of his heart alway.
Like two black Templars sit they there,
Beside one crupper, Knight and Care.

No knight am I with pennoned spear,
To prance upon a bold destrere:
I will not have black Care prevail
Upon my long-eared charger's tail,
For lo, I am a witless fool,
And laugh at Grief and ride a mule.

REQUIESCAT

Under the stone you behold,

Buried, and coffined, and cold,
Lieth Sir Wilfrid the Bold.

Always he marched in advance,
Warring in Flanders and France,
Doughty with sword and with lance.

Famous in Saracen fight,
Rode in his youth the good knight,
Scattering Paynims in flight.

Brian the Templar untrue,
Fairly in tourney he slew,
Saw Hierusalem too.

Now he is buried and gone,
Lying beneath the gray stone:
Where shall you find such a one?

Long time his widow deplored,
Weeping the fate of her lord,
Sadly cut off by the sword.

When she was eased of her pain,
Came the good Lord Athelstane,
When her ladyship married again.

LINES UPON MY SISTER'S PORTRAIT

BY THE LORD SOUTHDOWN

The castle towers of Bareacres are fair upon the lea,
Where the cliffs of bonny Diddlesex rise up from out the sea:
I stood upon the donjon keep and view'd the country o'er,
I saw the lands of Bareacres for fifty miles or more.
I stood upon the donjon keep—it is a sacred place,—
Where floated for eight hundred years the banner of my race;
Argent, a dexter sinople, and gules an azure field:
There ne'er was nobler cognizance on knightly warrior's shield.

The first time England saw the shield 'twas round a Norman neck,
On board a ship from Valery, King William was on deck.
A Norman lance the colors wore, in Hastings' fatal fray—
St. Willibald for Bareacres! 'twas double gules that day!
O Heaven and sweet St. Willibald! in many a battle since
A loyal-hearted Bareacres has ridden by his Prince!

At Acre with Plantagenet, with Edward at Poictiers,
The pennon of the Bareacres was foremost on the spears!

'Twas pleasant in the battle-shock to hear our war-cry ringing:
Oh grant me, sweet St. Willibald, to listen to such singing!
Three hundred steel-clad gentlemen, we drove the foe before us,
And thirty score of British bows kept twanging to the chorus!
O knights, my noble ancestors! and shall I never hear
St. Willibald for Bareacres through battle ringing clear?
I'd cut me off this strong right hand a single hour to ride,
And strike a blow for Bareacres, my fathers, at your side!

Dash down, dash down, yon Mandolin, beloved sister mine!
Those blushing lips may never sing the glories of our line:
Our ancient castles echo to the clumsy feet of churls,
The spinning-jenny houses in the mansion of our Earls.
Sing not, sing not, my Angeline! in days so base and vile,
'Twere sinful to be happy, 'twere sacrilege to smile.
I'll hie me to my lonely hall, and by its cheerless hob
I'll muse on other days, and wish—and wish I were—A SNOB.

THE LEGEND OF ST. SOPHIA OF KIOFF.

AN EPIC POEM, IN TWENTY BOOKS.

I.

[The Poet describes the city and spelling of Kiow, Kioff, or Kiova.]

A thousand years ago, or more,
A city filled with burghers stout,
And girt with ramparts round about,
Stood on the rocky Dnieper shore.
In armor bright, by day and night,
The sentries they paced to and fro.
Well guarded and walled was this town, and called
By different names, I'd have you to know;
For if you looks in the g'ography books,
In those dictionaries the name it varies,
And they write it off Kieff or Kioff, Kiova or Kiow.

II.

[Its buildings, public works, and ordinances, religious and civil.]

Thus guarded without by wall and redoubt,
Kiova within was a place of renown,
With more advantages than in those dark ages
Were commonly known to belong to a town.
There were places and squares, and each year four fairs,
And regular aldermen and regular lord-mayors;
And streets, and alleys, and a bishop's palace;
And a church with clocks for the orthodox—
With clocks and with spires, as religion desires;
And beadles to whip the bad little boys
Over their poor little corduroys,
In service-time, when they DIDN'T make a noise;
And a chapter and dean, and a cathedral-green
With ancient trees, underneath whose shades
Wandered nice young nursery-maids.

[The poet shows how a certain priest dwelt at Kioff, a godly clergyman, and one that preached rare good sermons.]

Ding-dong, ding-dong, ding-ding-a-ring-ding,
The bells they made a merry merry ring,
From the tall tall steeple; and all the people
(Except the Jews) came and filled the pews—
Poles, Russians and Germans,
To hear the sermons
Which HYACINTH preached godly to those Germans and Poles,
For the safety of their souls.

III.

[How this priest was short and fat of body;]

A worthy priest he was and a stout—
You've seldom looked on such a one;
For, though he fasted thrice in a week,
Yet nevertheless his skin was sleek;
His waist it spanned two yards about
And he weighed a score of stone.

IV.

[And like unto the author of "Plymley's Letters."]

A worthy priest for fasting and prayer
And mortification most deserving;
And as for preaching beyond compare,
He'd exert his powers for three or four hours,
With greater pith than Sydney Smith

Or the Reverend Edward Irving.

V.

[Of what convent he was prior, and when the convent was built.]

He was the prior of Saint Sophia
(A Cockney rhyme, but no better I know)—
Of St. Sophia, that Church in Kiow,
Built by missionaries I can't tell when;
Who by their discussions converted the Russians,
And made them Christian men.

VI.

[Of Saint Sophia of Kioff; and how her statue miraculously travelled thither.]

Sainted Sophia (so the legend vows)
With special favor did regard this house;
And to uphold her converts' new devotion
Her statue (needing but her legs for HER ship)
Walks of itself across the German Ocean;
And of a sudden perches
In this the best of churches,
Whither all Kiovites come and pay it grateful worship.

VII.

[And how Kioff should have been a happy city; but that]

Thus with her patron-saints and pious preachers
Recorded here in catalogue precise,
A goodly city, worthy magistrates,
You would have thought in all the Russian states
The citizens the happiest of all creatures,—
The town itself a perfect Paradise.

VIII.

[Certain wicked Cossacks did besiege it,]

No, alas! this well-built city
Was in a perpetual fidget;
For the Tartars, without pity,
Did remorselessly besiege it.

Tartars fierce, with sword and sabres,
Huns and Turks, and such as these,

Envied much their peaceful neighbors
By the blue Borysthenes.

[Murdering the citizens,]

Down they came, these ruthless Russians,
From their steppes, and woods, and fens,
For to levy contributions
On the peaceful citizens.

Winter, Summer, Spring, and Autumn,
Down they came to peaceful Kioff,
Killed the burghers when they caught 'em,
If their lives they would not buy off.

[Until they agreed to pay a tribute yearly.]

Till the city, quite confounded
By the ravages they made,
Humbly with their chief compounded,
And a yearly tribute paid.

[How they paid the tribute, and suddenly refused it,]

Which (because their courage lax was)
They discharged while they were able:
Tolerated thus the tax was,
Till it grew intolerable,

[To the wonder of the Cossack envoy.]

And the Calmuc envoy sent,
As before to take their dues all,
Got, to his astonishment,
A unanimous refusal!

[Of a mighty gallant speech]

"Men of Kioff!" thus courageous
Did the stout lord-mayor harangue them,
"Wherefore pay these sneaking wages
To the hectoring Russians? hang them!

[That the lord-mayor made,]

"Hark! I hear the awful cry of
Our forefathers in their graves;
"'Fight, ye citizens of Kioff!

Kioff was not made for slaves.'

[Exhorting the burghers to pay no longer.]

"All too long have ye betrayed her;
Rouse, ye men and aldermen,
Send the insolent invader—
Send him starving back again."

IX.

[Of their thanks and heroic resolves.]

He spoke and he sat down; the people of the town,
Who were fired with a brave emulation,
Now rose with one accord, and voted thanks unto the lord-
Mayor for his oration:

[They dismiss the envoy, and set about drilling.]

The envoy they dismissed, never placing in his fist
So much as a single shilling;
And all with courage fired, as his lordship he desired,
At once set about their drilling.

[Of the City guard: viz. Militia, dragoons, and bombardiers, and their commanders.]

Then every city ward established a guard,
Diurnal and nocturnal:
Militia volunteers, light dragoons, and bombardiers,
With an alderman for colonel.

[Of the majors and captains.]

There was muster and roll-calls, and repairing city walls,
And filling up of fosses:
And the captains and the majors, gallant and courageous,
A-riding about on their hosses.

[The fortifications and artillery.]

To be guarded at all hours they built themselves watch-towers,
With every tower a man on;
And surely and secure, each from out his embrasure,
Looked down the iron cannon!

[Of the conduct of the actors and the clergy.]

A battle-song was writ for the theatre, where it
Was sung with vast enérgy
And rapturous applause; and besides, the public cause,
Was supported by the clergy.

The pretty ladies'-maids were pinning of cockades,
And tying on of sashes;
And dropping gentle tears, while their lovers bluster'd fierce,
About gunshot and gashes;

[Of the ladies;]

The ladies took the hint, and all day were scraping lint,
As became their softer genders;
And got bandages and beds for the limbs and for the heads
Of the city's brave defenders.

[And, finally, of the taylors.]

The men, both young and old, felt resolute and bold,
And panted hot for glory;
Even the tailors 'gan to brag, and embroidered on their flag,
"AUT WINCERE AUT MORI."

X.

[Of the Cossack chief,—his stratagem;]

Seeing the city's resolute condition,
The Cossack chief, too cunning to despise it,
Said to himself, "Not having ammunition
Wherewith to batter the place in proper form,
Some of these nights I'll carry it by storm,
And sudden escalade it or surprise it.

[And the burghers' sillie victorie.]

"Let's see, however, if the cits stand firmish."
He rode up to the city gates; for answers,
Out rushed an eager troop of the town élite,
And straightway did begin a gallant skirmish:
The Cossack hereupon did sound retreat,
Leaving the victory with the city lancers.

[What prisoners they took,]

They took two prisoners and as many horses,
And the whole town grew quickly so elate

With this small victory of their virgin forces,
That they did deem their privates and commanders
So many Caesars, Pompeys, Alexanders,
Napoleons, or Fredericks the Great.

[And how conceited they were.]

And puffing with inordinate conceit
They utterly despised these Cossack thieves;
And thought the ruffians easier to beat
Than porters carpets think, or ushers boys.
Meanwhile, a sly spectator of their joys,
The Cossack captain giggled in his sleeves.

[Of the Cossack chief,—his orders;]

"Whene'er you meet yon stupid city hogs."
(He bade his troops precise this order keep),
"Don't stand a moment—run away, you dogs!"
'Twas done; and when they met the town battalions,
The Cossacks, as if frightened at their valiance,
Turned tail, and bolted like so many sheep.

[And how he feigned a retreat.]

They fled, obedient to their captain's order:
And now this bloodless siege a month had lasted,
When, viewing the country round, the city warder
(Who, like a faithful weathercock, did perch
Upon the steeple of St. Sophy's church),
Sudden his trumpet took, and a mighty blast he blasted.

[The warder proclayms the Cossacks' retreat, and the citie greatly rejoyces.]

His voice it might be heard through all the streets
(He was a warder wondrous strong in lung),
"Victory, victory! the foe retreats!"
"The foe retreats!" each cries to each he meets;
"The foe retreats!" each in his turn repeats.
Gods! how the guns did roar, and how the joy-bells rung!

Arming in haste his gallant city lancers,
The mayor, to learn if true the news might be,
A league or two out issued with his prancers.
The Cossacks (something had given their courage a damper)
Hastened their flight, and 'gan like mad to scamper:
Blessed be all the saints, Kiova town was free!

XI.

Now, puffed with pride, the mayor grew vain,
Fought all his battles o'er again;
And thrice he routed all his foes, and thrice he slew the slain.
'Tis true he might amuse himself thus,
And not be very murderous;
For as of those who to death were done
The number was exactly NONE,
His lordship, in his soul's elation,
Did take a bloodless recreation—

[The manner of the citie's rejoycings,]

Going home again, he did ordain
A very splendid cold collation
For the magistrates and the corporation;
Likewise a grand illumination,
For the amusement of the nation.
That night the theatres were free,
The conduits they ran Malvolsie;
Each house that night did beam with light
And sound with mirth and jollity;

[And its impiety.]

But shame, O shame! not a soul in the town,
Now the city was safe and the Cossacks flown,
Ever thought of the bountiful saint by whose care
The town had been rid of these terrible Turks—
Said even a prayer to that patroness fair,
For these her wondrous works!

[How the priest, Hyacinth, waited at church, and nobody came thither.]

Lord Hyacinth waited, the meekest of priors—
He waited at church with the rest of his friars;
He went there at noon and he waited till ten,
Expecting in vain the lord-mayor and his men.
He waited and waited from mid-day to dark;
But in vain—you might search through the whole of the church,
Not a layman, alas! to the city's disgrace,
From mid-day to dark showed his nose in the place.
The pew-woman, organist, beadle, and clerk,
Kept away from their work, and were dancing like mad
Away in the streets with the other mad people,
Not thinking to pray, but to guzzle and tipple
Wherever the drink might be had.

XII.

[How he went forth to bid them to prayer.]

Amidst this din and revelry throughout the city roaring,
The silver moon rose silently, and high in heaven soaring;
Prior Hyacinth was fervently upon his knees adoring:
"Towards my precious patroness this conduct sure unfair is;
I cannot think, I must confess, what keeps the dignitaries
And our good mayor away, unless some business them contraries."
He puts his long white mantle on and forth the prior sallies—
(His pious thoughts were bent upon good deeds and not on malice):
Heavens! how the banquet lights they shone about the mayor's palace!

[How the grooms and lackeys jeered him.]

About the hall the scullions ran with meats both and fresh and potted;
The pages came with cup and can, all for the guests allotted;
Ah, how they jeered that good fat man as up the stairs he trotted!

He entered in the ante-rooms where sat the mayor's court in;
He found a pack of drunken grooms a-dicing and a-sporting;
The horrid wine and 'bacco fumes, they set the prior a-snorting!
The prior thought he'd speak about their sins before he went hence,
And lustily began to shout of sin and of repentance;
The rogues, they kicked the prior out before he'd done a sentence!

And having got no portion small of buffeting and tussling,
At last he reached the banquet-hall, where sat the mayor a-guzzling,
And by his side his lady tall dressed out in white sprig muslin.

[And the mayor, mayoress, and aldermen, being tipsie refused to go church.]

Around the table in a ring the guests were drinking heavy;
They'd drunk the church, and drunk the king, and the army and the navy;
In fact they'd toasted everything. The prior said, "God save ye!"

The mayor cried, "Bring a silver cup—there's one upon the beaufét;
And, Prior, have the venison up—it's capital rechauffé.
And so, Sir Priest, you've come to sup? And pray you, how's Saint Sophy?"
The prior's face quite red was grown, with horror and with anger;
He flung the proffered goblet down—it made a hideous clangor;
And 'gan a-preaching with a frown—he was a fierce haranguer.

He tried the mayor and aldermen—they all set up a-jeering:
He tried the common-councilmen—they too began a-sneering;
He turned towards the may'ress then, and hoped to get a hearing.

He knelt and seized her dinner-dress, made of the muslin snowy,
"To church, to church, my sweet mistress!" he cried; "the way I'll show ye."
Alas, the lady-mayoress fell back as drunk as Chloe!

XIII.

[How the prior went back alone.]

Out from this dissolute and drunken court
Went the good prior, his eyes with weeping dim:
He tried the people of a meaner sort—
They too, alas, were bent upon their sport,
And not a single soul would follow him!
But all were swigging schnaps and guzzling beer.

He found the cits, their daughters, sons, and spouses,
Spending the live-long night in fierce carouses:
Alas, unthinking of the danger near!
One or two sentinels the ramparts guarded,
The rest were sharing in the general feast:
"God wot, our tipsy town is poorly warded;
Sweet Saint Sophia help us!" cried the priest.

Alone he entered the cathedral gate,
Careful he locked the mighty oaken door;
Within his company of monks did wait,
A dozen poor old pious men—no more.
Oh, but it grieved the gentle prior sore,
To think of those lost souls, given up to drink and fate!

[And shut himself into Saint Sophia's chapel with his brethren.]

The mighty outer gate well barred and fast,
The poor old friars stirred their poor old bones,
And pattering swiftly on the damp cold stones,
They through the solitary chancel passed.
The chancel walls looked black and dim and vast,
And rendered, ghost-like, melancholy tones.

Onward the fathers sped, till coming nigh a
Small iron gate, the which they entered quick at,
They locked and double-locked the inner wicket
And stood within the chapel of Sophia.
Vain were it to describe this sainted place,
Vain to describe that celebrated trophy,
The venerable statue of Saint Sophy,
Which formed its chiefest ornament and grace.

Here the good prior, his personal griefs and sorrows
In his extreme devotion quickly merging,
At once began to pray with voice sonorous;
The other friars joined in pious chorus,
And passed the night in singing, praying, scourging,
In honor of Sophia, that sweet virgin.

XIV.

[The episode of Sneezoff and Katinka.]

Leaving thus the pious priest in
Humble penitence and prayer,
And the greedy cits a-feasting,
Let us to the walls repair.

Walking by the sentry-boxes,
Underneath the silver moon,
Lo! the sentry boldly cocks his—
Boldly cocks his musketoon.

Sneezoff was his designation,
Fair-haired boy, for ever pitied;
For to take his cruel station,
He but now Katinka quitted.

Poor in purse were both, but rich in
Tender love's delicious plenties;
She a damsel of the kitchen,
He a haberdasher's 'prentice.

'Tinka, maiden tender-hearted,
Was dissolved in tearful fits,
On that fatal night she parted
From her darling, fair-haired Fritz.

Warm her soldier lad she wrapt in
Comforter and muffettee;
Called him "general" and "captain,"
Though a simple private he.

"On your bosom wear this plaster,
'Twill defend you from the cold;
In your pipe smoke this canaster,
Smuggled 'tis, my love, and old.

"All the night, my love, I'll miss you."
Thus she spoke; and from the door

Fair-haired Sneezoff made his issue,
To return, alas, no more.

He it is who calmly walks his
Walk beneath the silver moon;
He it is who boldly cocks his
Detonating musketoon.

He the bland canaster puffing,
As upon his round he paces,
Sudden sees a ragamuffin
Clambering swiftly up the glacis.

"Who goes there?" exclaims the sentry;
"When the sun has once gone down
No one ever makes an entry
Into this here fortified town!"

[How the sentrie Sneezoff was surprised and slayn.]

Shouted thus the watchful Sneezoff;
But, ere any one replied,
Wretched youth! he fired his piece off
Started, staggered, groaned, and died!

XV.

[How the Cossacks rushed in suddenly and took the citie.]

Ah, full well might the sentinel cry, "Who goes there!"
But echo was frightened too much to declare.
Who goes there? who goes there? Can any one swear
To the number of sands sur les bords de la mer,
Or the whiskers of D'Orsay Count down to a hair?
As well might you tell of the sands the amount,
Or number each hair in each curl of the Count,
As ever proclaim the number and name
Of the hundreds and thousands that up the wall came!

[Of the Cossack troops,]

Down, down the knaves poured with fire and with sword:
There were thieves from the Danube and rogues from the Don;
There were Turks and Wallacks, and shouting Cossacks;
Of all nations and regions, and tongues and religions—
Jew, Christian, Idolater, Frank, Mussulman:
Ah, horrible sight was Kioff that night!

[And of their manner of burning, murdering, and ravishing.]

The gates were all taken—no chance e'en of flight;
And with torch and with axe the bloody Cossacks
Went hither and thither a-hunting in packs:
They slashed and they slew both Christian and Jew—
Women and children, they slaughtered them too.
Some, saving their throats, plunged into the moats,
Or the river—but oh, they had burned all the boats!

[How they burned the whole citie down, save the church,]

But here let us pause—for I can't pursue further
This scene of rack, ravishment, ruin, and murther.
Too well did the cunning old Cossack succeed!
His plan of attack was successful indeed!
The night was his own—the town it was gone;
'Twas a heap still a-burning of timber and stone.

[Whereof the bells began to ring.]

One building alone had escaped from the fires,
Saint Sophy's fair church, with its steeples and spires,
Calm, stately, and white,
It stood in the light;
And as if 'twould defy all the conqueror's power,—
As if nought had occurred,
Might clearly be heard
The chimes ringing soberly every half-hour!

XVI.

The city was defunct—silence succeeded
Unto its last fierce agonizing yell;
And then it was the conqueror first heeded
The sound of these calm bells.

[How the Cossack chief bade them burn the church too.]

Furious towards his aides-de-camp he turns,
And (speaking as if Byron's works he knew)
"Villains!" he fiercely cries, "the city burns,
Why not the temple too?
Burn me yon church, and murder all within!"

[How they stormed it, and of Hyacinth, his anger thereat.]

The Cossacks thundered at the outer door;

And Father Hyacinth, who, heard the din,
(And thought himself and brethren in distress,
Deserted by their lady patroness)
Did to her statue turn, and thus his woes outpour.

XVII.

[His prayer to the Saint Sophia.]

"And is it thus, O falsest of the saints,
Thou hearest our complaints?
Tell me, did ever my attachment falter
To serve thy altar?
Was not thy name, ere ever I did sleep,
The last upon my lip?
Was not thy name the very first that broke
From me when I awoke?
Have I not tried with fasting, flogging, penance,
And mortified counténance
For to find favor, Sophy, in thy sight?
And lo! this night,
Forgetful of my prayers, and thine own promise,
Thou turnest from us;
Lettest the heathen enter in our city,
And, without pity,
Murder out burghers, seize upon their spouses,
Burn down their houses!
Is such a breach of faith to be endured?
See what a lurid
Light from the insolent invader's torches
Shines on your porches!
E'en now, with thundering battering-ram and hammer
And hideous clamor;
With axemen, swordsmen, pikemen, billmen, bowmen,
The conquering foemen,
O Sophy! beat your gate about your ears,
Alas! and here's
A humble company of pious men,
Like muttons in a pen,
Whose souls shall quickly from their bodies be thrusted,
Because in you they trusted.
Do you not know the Calmuc chiefs desires—
KILL ALL THE FRIARS!
And you, of all the saints most false and fickle,
Leave us in this abominable pickle."

[The statue suddenlie speaks;]

"RASH HYACINTHUS!"
(Here, to the astonishment of all her backers,
Saint Sophy, opening wide her wooden jaws,
Like to a pair of German walnut-crackers,
Began), "I did not think you had been thus,—
O monk of little faith! Is it because
A rascal scum of filthy Cossack heathen
Besiege our town, that you distrust in ME, then?
Think'st thou that I, who in a former day
Did walk across the Sea of Marmora
(Not mentioning, for shortness, other seas),—
That I, who skimmed the broad Borysthenes,
Without so much as wetting of my toes,
Am frightened at a set of men like THOSE?
I have a mind to leave you to your fate:
Such cowardice as this my scorn inspires."

[But is interrupted by the breaking in of the Cossacks.]

Saint Sophy was here
Cut short in her words,—
For at this very moment in tumbled the gate,
And with a wild cheer,
And a clashing of swords,
Swift through the church porches,
With a waving of torches,
And a shriek and a yell
Like the devils of hell,
With pike and with axe
In rushed the Cossacks,—
In rushed the Cossacks, crying,
"MURDER THE FRIARS!"

[Of Hyacinth, his outrageous address;]

Ah! what a thrill felt Hyacinth,
When he heard that villanous shout Calmuc!
Now, thought he, my trial beginneth;
Saints, O give me courage and pluck!
"Courage, boys, 'tis useless to funk!"
Thus unto the friars he began:
"Never let it be said that a monk
Is not likewise a gentleman.
Though the patron saint of the church,
Spite of all that we've done and we've pray'd,
Leaves us wickedly here in the lurch,
Hang it, gentlemen, who's afraid!"

[And preparation for dying.]

As thus the gallant Hyacinthus spoke,
He, with an air as easy and as free as
If the quick-coming murder were a joke,
Folded his robes around his sides, and took
Place under sainted Sophy's legs of oak,
Like Caesar at the statue of Pompeius.
The monks no leisure had about to look
(Each being absorbed in his particular case),
Else had they seen with what celestial race
A wooden smile stole o'er the saint's mahogany face.

[Saint Sophia, her speech.]

"Well done, well done, Hyacinthus, my son!"
Thus spoke the sainted statue.
"Though you doubted me in the hour of need,
And spoke of me very rude indeed,
You deserve good luck for showing such pluck,
And I won't be angry at you."

[She gets on the prior's shoulder straddle-back,]

The monks by-standing, one and all,
Of this wondrous scene beholders,
To this kind promise listened content,
And couldn't contain their astonishment,
When Saint Sophia moved and went
Down from her wooden pedestal,
And twisted her legs, sure as eggs is eggs,
Round Hyacinthus's shoulders!

[And bids him run.]

"Ho! forwards," cried Sophy, "there's no time for waiting,
The Cossacks are breaking the very last gate in:
See the glare of their torches shines red through the grating;
We've still the back door, and two minutes or more.
Now boys, now or never, we must make for the river,
For we only are safe on the opposite shore.
Run swiftly to-day, lads, if ever you ran,—
Put out your best leg, Hyacinthus, my man;
And I'll lay five to two that you carry us through,
Only scamper as fast as you can."

XVIII.

[He runneth,]

Away went the priest through the little back door,
And light on his shoulders the image he bore:
The honest old priest was not punished the least,
Though the image was eight feet, and he measured four.
Away went the prior, and the monks at his tail
Went snorting, and puffing, and panting full sail;
And just as the last at the back door had passed,
In furious hunt behold at the front
The Tartars so fierce, with their terrible cheers;
With axes, and halberts, and muskets, and spears,
With torches a-flaming the chapel now came in.
They tore up the mass-book, they stamped on the psalter,
They pulled the gold crucifix down from the altar;
The vestments they burned with their blasphemous fires,
And many cried, "Curse on them! where are the friars?"
When loaded with plunder, yet seeking for more,
One chanced to fling open the little back door,
Spied out the friars' white robes and long shadows
In the moon, scampering over the meadows,
And stopped the Cossacks in the midst of their arsons,
By crying out lustily, "THERE GO THE PARSONS!"

[And the Tartars after him.]

With a whoop and a yell, and a scream and a shout,
At once the whole murderous body turned out;
And swift as the hawk pounces down on the pigeon,
Pursued the poor short-winded men of religion.

[How the friars sweated.]

When the sound of that cheering came to the monks' hearing,
O heaven! how the poor fellows panted and blew!
At fighting not cunning, unaccustomed to running,
When the Tartars came up, what the deuce should they do?
"They'll make us all martyrs, those bloodthirsty Tartars!"
Quoth fat Father Peter to fat Father Hugh.
The shouts they came clearer, the foe they drew nearer;
Oh, how the bolts whistled, and how the lights shone!
"I cannot get further, this running is murther;
Come carry me, some one!" cried big Father John.
And even the statue grew frightened, "Od rat you!"
It cried, "Mr. Prior, I wish you'd get on!"
On tugged the good friar, but nigher and nigher
Appeared the fierce Russians, with sword and with fire.
On tugged the good prior at Saint Sophy's desire,—

A scramble through bramble, through mud, and through mire,
The swift arrows' whizziness causing a dizziness,
Nigh done his business, fit to expire.

[And the pursuers fixed arrows into their tayles.]

Father Hyacinth tugged, and the monks they tugged after:
The foemen pursued with a horrible laughter,
And hurl'd their long spears round the poor brethren's ears,
So true, that next day in the coats of each priest,
Though never a wound was given, there were found
A dozen arrows at least.

[How at the last gasp,]

Now the chase seemed at its worst,
Prior and monks were fit to burst;
Scarce you knew the which was first,
Or pursuers or pursued;
When the statue, by heaven's grace,
Suddenly did change the face
Of this interesting race,
As a saint, sure, only could.

For as the jockey who at Epsom rides,
When that his steed is spent and punished sore,
Diggeth his heels into the courser's sides,
And thereby makes him run one or two furlongs more;
Even thus, betwixt the eighth rib and the ninth,
The saint rebuked the prior, that weary creeper;
Fresh strength into his limbs her kicks imparted,
One bound he made, as gay as when he started.

[The friars won, and jumped into Borysthenes fluvius.]

Yes, with his brethren clinging at his cloak,
The statue on his shoulders—fit to choke—
One most tremendous bound made Hyacinth,
And soused friars, statue, and all, slap-dash into the Dnieper!

XIX.

[And how the Russians saw]

And when the Russians, in a fiery rank,
Panting and fierce, drew up along the shore;
(For here the vain pursuing they forbore,
Nor cared they to surpass the river's bank,)

Then, looking from the rocks and rushes dank,
A sight they witnessed never seen before,
And which, with its accompaniments glorious,
Is writ i' the golden book, or liber aureus.

[The statue get off Hyacinth his back, and sit down with the friars on Hyacinth his cloak.]

Plump in the Dnieper flounced the friar and friends—
They dangling round his neck, he fit to choke.
When suddenly his most miraculous cloak
Over the billowy waves itself extends,
Down from his shoulders quietly descends
The venerable Sophy's statue of oak;
Which, sitting down upon the cloak so ample,
Bids all the brethren follow its example!

[How in this manner of boat they sayled away.]

Each at her bidding sat, and sat at ease;
The statue 'gan a gracious conversation,
And (waving to the foe a salutation)
Sail'd with her wondering happy protégés
Gayly adown the wide Borysthenes,
Until they came unto some friendly nation.
And when the heathen had at length grown shy of
Their conquest, she one day came back again to Kioff.

XX.

[Finis, or the end.]

THINK NOT, O READER, THAT WE'RE LAUGHING AT YOU;
YOU MAY GO TO KIOFF NOW, AND SEE THE STATUTE!

TITMARSH'S CARMEN LILLIENSE.

LILLE, Sept. 2, 1843.

My heart is weary, my peace is gone,
How shall I e'er my woes reveal?
I have no money, I lie in pawn,
A stranger in the town of Lille.

I.
With twenty pounds but three weeks since

From Paris forth did Titmarsh wheel,
I thought myself as rich a prince
As beggar poor I'm now at Lille.

Confiding in my ample means—
In troth, I was a happy chiel!
I passed the gates of Valenciennes,
I never thought to come by Lille.

I never thought my twenty pounds
Some rascal knave would dare to steal;
I gayly passed the Belgic bounds
At Quiévrain, twenty miles from Lille.

To Antwerp town I hasten'd post,
And as I took my evening meal
I felt my pouch,—my purse was lost,
O Heaven! Why came I not by Lille?

I straightway called for ink and pen,
To grandmamma I made appeal;
Meanwhile a loan of guineas ten
I borrowed from a friend so leal.

I got the cash from grandmamma
(Her gentle heart my woes could feel,)
But where I went, and what I saw,
What matters? Here I am at Lille.

My heart is weary, my peace is gone,
How shall I e'er my woes reveal?
I have no cash, I lie in pawn,
A stranger in the town of Lille.

II.
To stealing I can never come,
To pawn my watch I'm too genteel,
Besides, I left my watch at home,
How could I pawn it then at Lille?

"La note," at times the guests will say.
I turn as white as cold boil'd veal;
I turn and look another way,
I dare not ask the bill at Lille.

I dare not to the landlord say,
"Good sir, I cannot pay your bill;"
He thinks I am a Lord Anglais,

And is quite proud I stay at Lille.

He thinks I am a Lord Anglais,
Like Rothschild or Sir Robert Peel,
And so he serves me every day
The best of meat and drink in Lille.

Yet when he looks me in the face
I blush as red as cochineal;
And think did he but know my case,
How changed he'd be, my host of Lille.

My heart is weary, my peace is gone,
How shall I e'er my woes reveal?
I have no money, I lie in pawn,
A stranger in the town of Lille.

III.
The sun bursts out in furious blaze,
I perspirate from head to heel;
I'd like to hire a one-horse chaise,
How can I, without cash at Lille?

I pass in sunshine burning hot
By cafés where in beer they deal;
I think how pleasant were a pot,
A frothing pot of beer of Lille!

What is yon house with walls so thick,
All girt around with guard and grille?
O gracious gods! it makes me sick,
It is the PRISON-HOUSE of Lille!

O cursed prison strong and barred,
It does my very blood congeal!
I tremble as I pass the guard,
And quit that ugly part of Lille.

The church-door beggar whines and prays,
I turn away at his appeal
Ah, church-door beggar! go thy ways!
You're not the poorest man in Lille.

My heart is weary, my peace is gone,
How shall I e'er any woes reveal?
I have no money, I lie in pawn,
A stranger in the town of Lille.
IV.

Say, shall I to you Flemish church,
And at a Popish altar kneel?
Oh, do not leave me in the lurch,—
I'll cry, ye patron-saints of Lille!

Ye virgins dressed in satin hoops,
Ye martyrs slain for mortal weal,
Look kindly down! before you stoops
The miserablest man in Lille.

And lo! as I beheld with awe
A pictured saint (I swear 'tis real),
It smiled, and turned to grandmamma!—
It did! and I had hope in Lille!

'Twas five o'clock, and I could eat,
Although I could not pay my meal:
I hasten back into the street
Where lies my inn, the best Lille.

What see I on my table stand,—
A letter with a well-known seal?
'Tis grandmamma's! I know her hand,—
"To Mr. M. A. Titmarsh, Lille."

I feel a choking in my throat,
I pant and stagger, faint and reel!
It is—it is—a ten-pound note,
And I'm no more in pawn at Lille!

[He goes off by the diligence that evening, and is restored to the bosom of his happy family.]

THE WILLOW-TREE

Know ye the willow-tree
Whose gray leaves quiver,
Whispering gloomily
To yon pale river;
Lady, at even-tide
Wander not near it,
They say its branches hide
A sad, lost spirit?

Once to the willow-tree
A maid came fearful,
Pale seemed her cheek to be,

Her blue eye tearful;
Soon as she saw the tree,
Her step moved fleeter,
No one was there—ah me!
No one to meet her!

Quick beat her heart to hear
The far bell's chime
Toll from the chapel-tower
The trysting time:
But the red sun went down
In golden flame,
And though she looked round,
Yet no one came!

Presently came the night,
Sadly to greet her,—
Moon in her silver light,
Stars in their glitter;
Then sank the moon away
Under the billow,
Still wept the maid alone—
There by the willow!

Through the long darkness,
By the stream rolling,
Hour after hour went on
Tolling and tolling.
Long was the darkness,
Lonely and stilly;
Shrill came the night-wind,
Piercing and chilly.

Shrill blew the morning breeze,
Biting and cold,
Bleak peers the gray dawn
Over the wold.
Bleak over moor and stream
Looks the grey dawn,
Gray, with dishevelled hair,
Still stands the willow there—
THE MAID IS GONE!

Domine, Domine!
Sing we a litany,—
Sing for poor maiden-hearts broken and weary;
Domine, Domine!
Sing we a litany,

Wail we and weep we a wild Miserere!

(ANOTHER VERSION).

I
Long by the willow-trees
Vainly they sought her,
Wild rang the mother's screams
O'er the gray water:
"Where is my lovely one?
Where is my daughter?

II
"Rouse thee, sir constable—
Rouse thee and look;
Fisherman, bring your net,
Boatman your hook.
Beat in the lily-beds,
Dive in the brook!"

III
Vainly the constable
Shouted and called her;
Vainly the fisherman
Beat the green alder,
Vainly he flung the net,
Never it hauled her!

IV
Mother beside the fire
Sat, her nightcap in;
Father, in easy chair,
Gloomily napping,
When at the window-sill
Came a light tapping!

V
And a pale countenance
Looked through the casement.
Loud beat the mother's heart,
Sick with amazement,
And at the vision which
Came to surprise her,
Shrieked in an agony—

"Lor! it's Elizar!"

VI
Yes, 'twas Elizabeth—
Yes, 'twas their girl;
Pale was her cheek, and her
Hair out of curl.
"Mother!" the loving one,
Blushing, exclaimed,
"Let not your innocent
Lizzy be blamed.

VII
"Yesterday, going to aunt
Jones's to tea,
Mother, dear mother, I
FORGOT THE DOOR-KEY!
And as the night was cold,
And the way steep,
Mrs. Jones kept me to
Breakfast and sleep."

VIII
Whether her Pa and Ma
Fully believed her,
That we shall never know,
Stern they received her;
And for the work of that
Cruel, though short, night,
Sent her to bed without
Tea for a fortnight.

IX
MORAL
Hey diddle diddlety,
Cat and the Fiddlety,
Maidens of England take caution by she!
Let love and suicide
Never tempt you aside,
And always remember to take the door-key.

LYRA HIBERNICA

THE POEMS OF THE MOLONY OF KILBALLYMOLONY

THE PIMLICO PAVILION

Ye pathrons of Janius, Minerva and Vanius,
Who sit on Parnassus, that mountain of snow,
Descind from your station and make observation
Of the Prince's pavilion in sweet Pimlico.

This garden, by jakurs, is forty poor acres,
(The garner he tould me, and sure ought to know;)
And yet greatly bigger, in size and in figure,
Than the Phanix itself, seems the Park Pimlico.

O 'tis there that the spoort is, when the Queen and the Court is
Walking magnanimous all of a row,
Forgetful what state is among the pataties
And the pine-apple gardens of sweet Pimlico.

There in blossoms odorous the birds sing a chorus,
Of "God save the Queen" as they hop to and fro;
And you sit on the binches and hark to the finches,
Singing melodious in sweet Pimlico.

There shuiting their phanthasies, they pluck polyanthuses
That round in the gardens resplindently grow,
Wid roses and jessimins, and other sweet specimins,
Would charm bould Linnayus in sweet Pimlico.

You see when you inther, and stand in the cinther,
Where the roses, and necturns, and collyflowers blow,
A hill so tremindous, it tops the top-windows
Of the elegant houses of famed Pimlico.

And when you've ascinded that precipice splindid
You see on its summit a wondtherful show—
A lovely Swish building, all painting and gilding,
The famous Pavilion of sweet Pimlico.

Prince Albert, of Flandthers, that Prince of Commandthers,
(On whom my best blessings hereby I bestow,)
With goold and vermilion has decked that Pavilion,
Where the Queen may take tay in her sweet Pimlico.

There's lines from John Milton the chamber all gilt on,
And pictures beneath them that's shaped like a bow;
I was greatly astounded to think that that Roundhead
Should find an admission to famed Pimlico.

O lovely's each fresco, and most picturesque O;
And while round the chamber astonished I go,

I think Dan Maclise's it baits all the pieces
Surrounding the cottage of famed Pimlico.

Eastlake has the chimney, (a good one to limn he,)
And a vargin he paints with a sarpent below;
While bulls, pigs, and panthers, and other enchanthers,
Are painted by Landseer in sweet Pimlico.

And nature smiles opposite, Stanfield he copies it;
O'er Claude or Poussang sure 'tis he that may crow:
But Sir Ross's best faiture is small mini-áture—
He shouldn't paint frescoes in famed Pimlico.

There's Leslie and Uwins has rather small doings;
There's Dyce, as brave masther as England can show;
And the flowers and the sthrawherries, sure he no dauber is,
That painted the panels of famed Pimlico.

In the pictures from Walther Scott, never a fault there's got,
Sure the marble's as natural as thrue Scaglio;
And the Chamber Pompayen is sweet to take tay in,
And ait butther'd muffins in sweet Pimlico.

There's landscapes by Gruner, both solar and lunar,
Them two little Doyles too, deserve a bravo;
Wid de piece by young Townsend, (for janins abounds in't;)
And that's why he's shuited to paint Pimlico.

That picture of Severn's is worthy of rever'nce,
But some I won't mintion is rather so so;
For sweet philoso'phy, or crumpets and coffee,
O where's a Pavilion like sweet Pimlico?

O to praise this Pavilion would puzzle Quintilian,
Daymosthenes, Brougham, or young Cicero;
So heavenly Goddess, d'ye pardon my modesty,
And silence, my lyre! about sweet Pimlico.

THE CRYSTAL PALACE

With ganial foire
Thransfuse me loyre,
Ye sacred nympths of Pindus,
The whoile I sing
That wondthrous thing,
The Palace made o' windows!

Say, Paxton, truth,
Thou wondthrous youth,
What sthroke of art celistial,
What power was lint
You to invint
This combineetion cristial.

O would before
That Thomas Moore,
Likewoise the late Lord Boyron,
Thim aigles sthrong
Of godlike song,
Cast oi on that cast oiron!

And saw thim walls,
And glittering halls,
Thim rising slendther columns,
Which I poor pote,
Could not denote,
No, not in twinty vollums.

My Muse's words
Is like the bird's
That roosts beneath the panes there;
Her wing she spoils
'Gainst them bright toiles,
And cracks her silly brains there.

This Palace tall,
This Cristial Hall,
Which Imperors might covet,
Stands in High Park
Like Noah's Ark,
A rainbow bint above it.

The towers and fanes,
In other scaynes,
The fame of this will undo,
Saint Paul's big doom,
Saint Payther's Room,
And Dublin's proud Rotundo.

'Tis here that roams,
As well becomes
Her dignitee and stations,
Victoria Great,
And houlds in state

The Congress of the Nations.

Her subjects pours
From distant shores,
Her Injians and Canajians;
And also we,
Her kingdoms three,
Attind with our allagiance.

Here come likewise
Her bould allies,
Both Asian and Europian;
From East and West
They send their best
To fill her Coornucopean.

I seen (thank Grace!)
This wonthrous place
(His Noble Honor Misther
H. Cole it was
That gave the pass,
And let me see what is there).

With conscious proide
I stud insoide
And look'd the World's Great Fair in,
Until me sight
Was dazzled quite,
And couldn't see for staring.

There's holy saints
And window paints,
By Maydiayval Pugin;
Alhamborough Jones
Did paint the tones
Of yellow and gambouge in.

There's fountains there
And crosses fair;
There's water-gods with urrns:
There's organs three,
To play, d'ye see?
"God save the Queen," by turrns.

There's Statues bright
Of marble white,
Of silver, and of copper;
And some in zinc,

And some, I think,
That isn't over proper.

There's staym Ingynes,
That stands in lines,
Enormous and amazing,
That squeal and snort
Like whales in sport,
Or elephants a-grazing.

There's carts and gigs,
And pins for pigs,
There's dibblers and there's harrows.
And ploughs like toys
For little boys,
And ilegant wheelbarrows.

For thim genteels
Who ride on wheels,
There's plenty to indulge 'em:
There's Droskys snug
From Paytersbug,
And vayhycles from Bulgium.

There's Cabs on Stands
And Shandthry danns;
There's Waggons from New York here;
There's Lapland Sleighs
Have cross'd the seas,
And Jaunting Cyars from Cork here.

Amazed I pass
From glass to glass,
Deloighted I survey 'em;
Fresh wondthers grows
Before me nose
In this sublime Musayum!

Look, here's a fan
From far Japan,
A sabre from Damasco:
There's shawls ye get
From far Thibet,
And cotton prints from Glasgow.

There's German flutes,
Marocky boots,
And Naples Macaronies;

Bohaymia
Has sent Bohay;
Polonia her polonies.

There's granite flints
That's quite imminse,
There's sacks of coals and fuels,
There's swords and guns,
And soap in tuns,
And Gingerbread and Jewels.

There's taypots there,
And cannons rare;
There's coffins fill'd with roses;
There's canvas tints,
Teeth insthrumints,
And shuits of clothes by MOSES.

There's lashins more
Of things in store,
But thim I don't remimber;
Nor could disclose
Did I compose
From May time to Novimber!

Ah, JUDY thru!
With eyes so blue,
That you were here to view it!
And could I screw
But tu pound tu,
'Tis I would thrait you to it!

So let us raise
Victoria's praise,
And Albert's proud condition,
That takes his ayse
As he surveys
This Cristial Exhibition.

1851.

MOLONY'S LAMENT

O Tim, did you hear of thim Saxons,
And read what the peepers report?
They're goan to recal the Liftinant,

And shut up the Castle and Coort!

Our desolate counthry of Oireland,
They're bint, the blagyards, to desthroy,
And now having murdthered our counthry,
They're goin to kill the Viceroy, Dear boy;
'Twas he was our proide and our joy!

And will we no longer behould him,
Surrounding his carriage in throngs,
As he weaves his cocked-hat from the windies,
And smiles to his bould aid-de-congs?
I liked for to see the young haroes,
All shoining with sthripes and with stars,
A horsing about in the Phaynix,
And winking the girls in the cyars,
Like Mars,
A smokin' their poipes and cigyars.

Dear Mitchell exoiled to Bermudies,
Your beautiful oilids you'll ope,
And there'll be an abondance of croyin'
From O'Brine at the Keep of Good Hope,
When they read of this news in the peepers,
Acrass the Atlantical wave,
That the last of the Oirish Liftinints
Of the oisland of Seents has tuck lave. God save
The Queen—she should betther behave.

And what's to become of poor Dame Sthreet,
And who'll ait the puffs and the tarts,
Whin the Coort of imparial splindor
From Doblin's sad city departs?
And who'll have the fiddlers and pipers,
When the deuce of a Coort there remains?
And where'll be the bucks and the ladies,
To hire the Coort-shuits and the thrains?
In sthrains,
It's thus that ould Erin complains!

There's Counsellor Flanagan's leedy
'Twas she in the Coort didn't fail,
And she wanted a plinty of popplin,
For her dthress, and her flounce, and her tail;
She bought it of Misthress O'Grady,
Eight shillings a yard tabinet,
But now that the Coort is concluded,
The divvle a yard will she get; I bet,

Bedad, that she wears the old set.

There's Surgeon O'Toole and Miss Leary,
They'd daylings at Madam O'Riggs';
Each year at the dthrawing-room sayson,
They mounted the neatest of wigs.
When Spring, with its buds and its dasies,
Comes out in her beauty and bloom,
Thim tu'll never think of new jasies,
Becase there is no dthrawing-room,
For whom
They'd choose the expense to ashume.

There's Alderman Toad and his lady,
'Twas they gave the Clart and the Poort,
And the poine-apples, turbots, and lobsters,
To feast the Lord Liftinint's Coort.
But now that the quality's goin,
I warnt that the aiting will stop,
And you'll get at the Alderman's teeble
The devil a bite or a dthrop,
Or chop;
And the butcher may shut up his shop.

Yes, the grooms and the ushers are goin,
And his Lordship, the dear honest man,
And the Duchess, his eemiable leedy,
And Corry, the bould Connellan,
And little Lord Hyde and the childthren,
And the Chewter and Governess tu;
And the servants are packing their boxes,—
Oh, murther, but what shall I due
Without you?
O Meery, with ois of the blue!

MR. MOLONY'S ACCOUNT OF THE BALL

GIVEN TO THE NEPAULESE AMBASSADOR BY THE PENINSULAR AND ORIENTAL COMPANY

O will ye choose to hear the news,
Bedad I cannot pass it o'er:
I'll tell you all about the Ball
To the Naypaulase Ambassador.
Begor! this fête all balls does bate
At which I've worn a pump, and I

Must here relate the splendthor great
Of th' Oriental Company.

These men of sinse dispoised expinse,
To fête these black Achilleses.
"We'll show the blacks," says they, "Almack's,
And take the rooms at Willis's."
With flags and shawls, for these Nepauls,
They hung the rooms of Willis up,
And decked the walls, and stairs, and halls,
With roses and with lilies up.

And Jullien's band it tuck its stand,
So sweetly in the middle there,
And soft bassoons played heavenly chunes,
And violins did fiddle there.
And when the Coort was tired of spoort,
I'd lave you, boys, to think there was
A nate buffet before them set,
Where lashins of good dhrink there was.

At ten before the ball-room door,
His moighty Excellincy was,
He smoiled and bowed to all the crowd,
So gorgeous and immense he was.
His dusky shuit, sublime and mute,
Into the door-way followed him;
And O the noise of the blackguard boys,
As they hurrood and hollowed him!

The noble Chair* stud at the stair,
And bade the dthrums to thump; and he
Did thus evince, to that Black Prince,
The welcome of his Company.
O fair the girls, and rich the curls,
And bright the oys you saw there, was;
And fixed each oye, ye there could spoi,
On Gineral Jung Bahawther, was!

This Gineral great then tuck his sate,
With all the other ginerals,
(Bedad his troat, his belt, his coat,
All bleezed with precious minerals;)
And as he there, with princely air,
Recloinin on his cushion was,
All round about his royal chair
The squeezin and the pushin was.

O Pat, such girls, such Jukes, and Earls,
Such fashion and nobilitee!
Just think of Tim, and fancy him
Amidst the hoigh gentilitee!
There was Lord De L'Huys, and the Portygeese
Ministher and his lady there,
And I reckonized, with much surprise,
Our messmate, Bob O'Grady, there;

There was Baroness Brunow, that looked like Juno,
And Baroness Rehausen there,
And Countess Roullier, that looked peculiar
Well, in her robes of gauze in there.
There was Lord Crowhurst (I knew him first,
When only Mr. Pips he was),
And Mick O'Toole, the great big fool,
That after supper tipsy was.

There was Lord Fingall, and his ladies all,
And Lords Killeen and Dufferin,
And Paddy Fife, with his fat wife:
I wondther how he could stuff her in.
There was Lord Belfast, that by me past,
And seemed to ask how should I go there?
And the Widow Macrae, and Lord A Hay,
And the Marchioness of Sligo there.

Yes, Jukes, and Earls, and diamonds, and pearls,
And pretty girls, was sporting there;
And some beside (the rogues!) I spied,
Behind the windies, coorting there.
O there's one I know, bedad would show
As beautiful as any there,
And I'd like to hear the pipers blow,
And shake a fut with Fanny there!

James Matheson, Esq., to whom, and the Board of Directors of the Peninsular and Oriental Company, I, Timotheus Molony, late stoker on board the "Iberia," the "Lady Mary Wood," the "Tagus," and the Oriental steamships, humbly dedicate this production of my grateful muse.

THE BATTLE OF LIMERICK

Ye Genii of the nation,
Who look with veneration.
And Ireland's desolation onsaysingly deplore;
Ye sons of General Jackson,

Who thrample on the Saxon,
Attend to the thransaction upon Shannon shore,

When William, Duke of Schumbug,
A tyrant and a humbug,
With cannon and with thunder on our city bore,
Our fortitude and valiance
Insthructed his battalions
To respict the galliant Irish upon Shannon shore.

Since that capitulation,
No city in this nation
So grand a reputation could boast before,
As Limerick prodigious,
That stands with quays and bridges,
And the ships up to the windies of the Shannon shore.

A chief of ancient line,
'Tis William Smith O'Brine
Reprisints this darling Limerick, this ten years or more:
O the Saxons can't endure
To see him on the flure,
And thrimble at the Cicero from Shannon shore!

This valliant son of Mars
Had been to visit Par's,
That land of Revolution, that grows the tricolor;
And to welcome his returrn
From pilgrimages furren,
We invited him to tay on the Shannon shore.

Then we summoned to our board
Young Meagher of the sword:
'Tis he will sheathe that battle-axe in Saxon gore;
And Mitchil of Belfast
We bade to our repast,
To dthrink a dish of coffee on the Shannon shore.

Convaniently to hould
These patriots so bould,
We tuck the opportunity of Tim Doolan's store;
And with ornamints and banners
(As becomes gintale good manners)
We made the loveliest tay-room upon Shannon shore.

'Twould binifit your sowls,
To see the butthered rowls,
The sugar-tongs and sangwidges and craim galyore,

And the muffins and the crumpets,
And the band of hearts and thrumpets,
To celebrate the sworry upon Shannon shore.

Sure the Imperor of Bohay
Would be proud to dthrink the tay
That Misthress Biddy Rooney for O'Brine did pour;
And, since the days of Strongbow,
There never was such Congo—
Mitchil dthrank six quarts of it—by Shannon shore.

But Clarndon and Corry
Connellan beheld this sworry
With rage and imulation in their black hearts' core;
And they hired a gang of ruffins
To interrupt the muffins,
And the fragrance of the Congo on the Shannon shore.

When full of tay and cake,
O'Brine began to spake;
But juice a one could hear him, for a sudden roar
Of a ragamuffin rout
Began to yell and shout,
And frighten the propriety of Shannon shore.

As Smith O'Brine harangued,
They batthered and they banged:
Tim Doolan's doors and windies down they tore;
They smashed the lovely windies
(Hung with muslin from the Indies),
Purshuing of their shindies upon Shannon shore.

With throwing of brickbats,
Drowned puppies and dead rats,
These ruffin democrats themselves did lower;
Tin kettles, rotten eggs,
Cabbage-stalks, and wooden legs,
They flung among the patriots of Shannon shore.

O the girls began to scrame
And upset the milk and crame;
And the honorable gintlemin, they cursed and swore:
And Mitchil of Belfast,
'Twas he that looked aghast,
When they roasted him in effigy by Shannon shore.

O the lovely tay was spilt
On that day of Ireland's guilt;

Says Jack Mitchil, "I am kilt! Boys, where's the back door?
'Tis a national disgrace:
Let me go and veil me face;"
And he boulted with quick pace from the Shannon shore.

"Cut down the bloody horde!"
Says Meagher of the sword,
"This conduct would disgrace any blackamore;"
But the best use Tommy made
Of his famous battle blade
Was to cut his own stick from the Shannon shore.

Immortal Smith O'Brine
Was raging like a line;
'Twould have done your sowl good to have heard him roar;
In his glory he arose,
And he rushed upon his foes,
But they hit him on the nose by the Shannon shore.

Then the Futt and the Dthragoons
In squadthrons and platoons,
With their music playing chunes, down upon us bore;
And they bate the rattatoo,
But the Peelers came in view,
And ended the shaloo on the Shannon shore.

LARRY O'TOOLE

You've all heard of Larry O'Toole,
Of the beautiful town of Drumgoole;
He had but one eye,
To ogle ye by—
Oh, murther, but that was a jew'l!
A fool
He made of de girls, dis O'Toole.

'Twas he was the boy didn't fail,
That tuck down pataties and mail;
He never would shrink
From any sthrong dthrink,
Was it whisky or Drogheda ale;
I'm bail
This Larry would swallow a pail.

Oh, many a night at the bowl,
With Larry I've sot cheek by jowl;

He's gone to his rest,
Where's there's dthrink of the best,
And so let us give his old sowl
A howl,
For 'twas he made the noggin to rowl.

THE ROSE OF FLORA

Sent by a Young Gentleman of Quality to Miss Br-dy, of Castle Brady.

On Brady's tower there grows a flower,
It is the loveliest flower that blows,—
At Castle Brady there lives a lady,
(And how I love her no one knows);
Her name is Nora, and the goddess Flora
Presents her with this blooming rose.

"O Lady Nora," says the goddess Flora,
"I've many a rich and bright parterre;
In Brady's towers there's seven more flowers,
But you're the fairest lady there:
Not all the county, nor Ireland's bounty,
Can projuice a treasure that's half so fair!"

What cheek is redder? sure roses fed her!
Her hair is maregolds, and her eye of blew.
Beneath her eyelid, is like the vi'let,
That darkly glistens with gentle jew!
The lily's nature is not surely whiter
Than Nora's neck is,—and her arrums too.

"Come, gentle Nora," says the goddess Flora,
"My dearest creature, take my advice,
There is a poet, full well you know it,
Who spends his lifetime in heavy sighs,—
Young Redmond Barry, 'tis him you'll marry,
If rhyme and raisin you'd choose likewise."

THE LAST IRISH GRIEVANCE

On reading of the general indignation occasioned in Ireland by the appointment of a Scotch Professor to one of HER MAJESTY'S Godless colleges, MASTER MOLLOY MOLONY, brother of THADDEUS MOLONY, Esq., of the Temple, a youth only fifteen years of age, dashed off the following spirited lines:—

As I think of the insult that's done to this nation,
Red tears of rivinge from me fatures I wash,
And uphold in this pome, to the world's daytistation,
The sleeves that appointed PROFESSOR M'COSH.

I look round me counthree, renowned by exparience,
And see midst her childthren, the witty, the wise,—
Whole hayps of logicians, potes, schollars, grammarians,
All ayger for pleeces, all panting to rise;

I gaze round the world in its utmost diminsion;
LARD JAHN and his minions in Council I ask;
Was there ever a Government-pleece (with a pinsion)
But children of Erin were fit for that task?

What, Erin beloved, is thy fetal condition?
What shame in aych boosom must rankle and burrun,
To think that our countree has ne'er a logician
In the hour of her deenger will surrev her turrun!

On the logic of Saxons there's little reliance,
And, rather from Saxons than gather its rules,
I'd stamp under feet the base book of his science,
And spit on his chair as he taught in the schools!

O false SIR JOHN KANE! is it thus that you praych me?
I think all your Queen's Universitees Bosh;
And if you've no neetive Professor to taych me,
I scawurn to be learned by the Saxon M'COSH.

There's WISEMAN and CHUME, and His Grace the Lord Primate,
That sinds round the box, and the world will subscribe;
'Tis they'll build a College that's fit for our climate,
And taych me the saycrets I burn to imboibe!

'Tis there as a Student of Science I'll enther,
Fair Fountain of Knowledge, of Joy, and Contint!
SAINT PATHRICK'S sweet Statue shall stand in the centher,
And wink his dear oi every day during Lint.

And good Doctor NEWMAN, that praycher unwary,
'Tis he shall preside the Academee School,
And quit the gay robe of ST. PHILIP of Neri,
To wield the soft rod of ST. LAWRENCE O'TOOLE!

An igstrawnary tail I vill tell you this veek—
I stood in the Court of A'Beckett the Beak,
Vere Mrs. Jane Roney, a vidow, I see,
Who charged Mary Brown with a robbin of she.

This Mary was pore and in misery once,
And she came to Mrs. Roney it's more than twelve monce.
She adn't got no bed, nor no dinner nor no tea,
And kind Mrs. Roney gave Mary all three.

Mrs. Roney kep Mary for ever so many veeks,
(Her conduct disgusted the best of all Beax,)
She kep her for nothink, as kind as could be,
Never thinkin that this Mary was a traitor to she.

"Mrs. Roney, O Mrs. Roney, I feel very ill;
Will you just step to the Doctor's for to fetch me a pill?"
"That I will, my pore Mary," Mrs. Roney says she;
And she goes off to the Doctor's as quickly as may be.

No sooner on this message Mrs. Roney was sped,
Than hup gits vicked Mary, and jumps out a bed;
She hopens all the trunks without never a key—
She bustes all the boxes, and vith them makes free.

Mrs. Roney's best linning, gownds, petticoats, and close,
Her children's little coats and things, her boots, and her hose,
She packed them, and she stole 'em, and avay vith them did flee.
Mrs. Roney's situation—you may think vat it vould be!

Of Mary, ungrateful, who had served her this vay,
Mrs. Roney heard nothink for a long year and a day.
Till last Thursday, in Lambeth, ven whom should she see
But this Mary, as had acted so ungrateful to she?

She was leaning on the helbo of a worthy young man,
They were going to be married, and were walkin hand in hand;
And the Church bells was a ringing for Mary and he,
And the parson was ready, and a waitin for his fee.

When up comes Mrs. Roney, and faces Mary Brown,
Who trembles, and castes her eyes upon the ground.
She calls a jolly pleaseman, it happens to be me;
I charge this yonng woman, Mr. Pleaseman, says she.

"Mrs. Roney, O, Mrs. Roney, O, do let me go,
I acted most ungrateful I own, and I know,
But the marriage bell is a ringin, and the ring you may see,
And this young man is a waitin," says Mary says she.

"I don't care three fardens for the parson and clark,
And the bell may keep ringin from noon day to dark.
Mary Brown, Mary Brown, you must come along with me;
And I think this young man is lucky to be free."

So, in spite of the tears which bejew'd Mary's cheek,
I took that young gurl to A'Beckett the Beak;
That exlent Justice demanded her plea—
But never a sullable said Mary said she.

On account of her conduck so base and so vile,
That wicked young gurl is committed for trile,
And if she's transpawted beyond the salt sea,
It's a proper reward for such willians as she.

Now you young gurls of Southwark for Mary who veep,
From pickin and stealin your ands you must keep,
Or it may be my dooty, as it was Thursday veek,
To pull you all hup to A'Beckett the Beak.

THE THREE CHRISTMAS WAITS

My name is Pleaceman X;
Last night I was in bed,
A dream did me perplex,
Which came into my Edd.
I dreamed I sor three Waits
A playing of their tune,
At Pimlico Palace gates,
All underneath the moon.
One puffed a hold French horn,
And one a hold Banjo,
And one chap seedy and torn
A Hirish pipe did blow.
They sadly piped and played,
Dexcribing of their fates;
And this was what they said,
Those three pore Christmas Waits:

"When this black year began,
This Eighteen-forty-eight,

I was a great great man,
And king both vise and great,
And Munseer Guizot by me did show
As Minister of State.

"But Febuwerry came,
And brought a rabble rout,
And me and my good dame
And children did turn out,
And us, in spite of all our right.
Sent to the right about.

"I left my native ground,
I left my kin and kith,
I left my royal crownd,
Vich I couldn't travel vith,
And without a pound came to English ground,
In the name of Mr. Smith.

"Like any anchorite
I've lived since I came here,
I've kep myself quite quite,
I've drank the small small beer,
And the vater, you see, disagrees vith me
And all my famly dear.

"O Tweeleries so dear,
O darling Pally Royl,
Vas it to finish here
That I did trouble and toyl?
That all my plans should break in my ands,
And should on me recoil?

"My state I fenced about
Vith baynicks and vith guns;
My gals I portioned hout,
Rich vives I got my sons;
O varn't it crule to lose my rule,
My money and lands at once?

"And so, vith arp and woice,
Both troubled and shagreened,
I hid you to rejoice,
O glorious England's Queend!
And never have to veep, like pore Louis-Phileep,
Because you out are cleaned.

"O Prins, so brave and stout,

I stand before your gate;
Pray send a trifle hout
To me, your pore old Vait;
For nothink could be vuss than it's been along vith us
In this year Forty-eight."

"Ven this bad year began,"
The nex man said, seysee,
"I vas a Journeyman,
A taylor black and free,
And my wife went out and chaired about,
And my name's the bold Cuffee.

"The Queen and Halbert both
I swore I would confound,
I took a hawfle hoath
To drag them to the ground;
And sevral more with me they swore
Aginst the British Crownd.

"Aginst her Pleacemen all
We said we'd try our strenth;
Her scarlick soldiers tall
We vow'd we'd lay full lenth;
And out we came, in Freedom's name,
Last Aypril was the tenth.

"Three 'undred thousand snobs
Came out to stop the vay,
Vith sticks vith iron knobs,
Or else we'd gained the day.
The harmy quite kept out of sight,
And so ve vent avay.

"Next day the Pleacemen came—
Rewenge it was their plann—
And from my good old dame
They took her tailor-mann:
And the hard hard beak did me bespeak
To Newgit in the Wann.

"In that etrocious Cort
The Jewry did agree;
The Judge did me transport,
To go beyond the sea:
And so for life, from his dear wife
They took poor old Cuffee.

"O Halbert, Appy Prince!
With children round your knees,
Ingraving ansum Prints,
And taking hoff your hease;
O think of me, the old Cuffee,
Beyond the solt solt seas!

"Although I'm hold and black,
My hanguish is most great;
Great Prince, O call me back,
And I vill be your Vait!
And never no more vill break the Lor,
As I did in 'Forty-eight."

The tailer thus did close
(A pore old blackymore rogue),
When a dismal gent uprose,
And spoke with Hirish brogue:
"I'm Smith O'Brine, of Royal Line,
Descended from Rory Ogue.

"When great O'Connle died,
That man whom all did trust,
That man whom Henglish pride
Beheld with such disgust,
Then Erin free fixed eyes on me,
And swoar I should be fust.

"'The glorious Hirish Crown,'
Says she, 'it shall be thine:
Long time, it's wery well known,
You kep it in your line;
That diadem of hemerald gem
Is yours, my Smith O'Brine.

"'Too long the Saxon churl
Our land encumbered hath;
Arise my Prince, my Earl,
And brush them from thy path:
Rise, mighty Smith, and sveep 'em vith
The besom of your wrath.'

"Then in my might I rose,
My country I surveyed,
I saw it filled with foes,
I viewed them undismayed;
'Ha, ha!' says I, 'the harvest's high,
I'll reap it with my blade.'

"My warriors I enrolled,
They rallied round their lord;
And cheafs in council old
I summoned to the board—
Wise Doheny and Duffy bold,
And Meagher of the Sword.

"I stood on Slievenamaun,
They came with pikes and bills;
They gathered in the dawn,
Like mist upon the hills,
And rushed adown the mountain side
Like twenty thousand rills.

"Their fortress we assail;
Hurroo! my boys, hurroo!
The bloody Saxons quail
To hear the wild Shaloo:
Strike, and prevail, proud Innesfail,
O'Brine aboo, aboo!

"Our people they defied;
They shot at 'em like savages,
Their bloody guns they plied
With sanguinary ravages:
Hide, blushing Glory, hide
That day among the cabbages!

"And so no more I'll say,
But ask your Mussy great.
And humbly sing and pray,
Your Majesty's poor Wait:
Your Smith O'Brine in 'Forty-nine
Will blush for 'Forty-eight."

LINES ON A LATE HOSPICIOUS EWENT.*

BY A GENTLEMAN OF THE FOOTGUARDS (BLUE)

I paced upon my beat
With steady step and slow,
All huppandownd of Ranelagh Street:
Ran'lagh St. Pimlico.

While marching huppandownd

Upon that fair May morn,
Beold the booming cannings sound,
A royal child is born!

The Ministers of State
Then presnly I sor,
They gallops to the Pallis gate,
In carridges and for.

With anxious looks intent,
Before the gate they stop,
There comes the good Lord President,
And there the Archbishopp.

Lord John he next elights;
And who comes here in haste?
'Tis the ero of one underd fights,
The caudle for to taste.

Then Mrs. Lily, the nuss,
Towards them steps with joy;
Says the brave old Duke, "Come tell to us,
Is it a gal or a boy?"

Says Mrs. L. to the Duke,
"Your Grace, it is A PRINCE."
And at that nuss's bold rebuke,
He did both laugh and wince.

He vews with pleasant look
This pooty flower of May,
Then, says the wenarable Duke,
"Egad, it's my buthday."

By memory backwards borne,
Peraps his thoughts did stray
To that old place where he was born,
Upon the first of May.

Perhaps he did recal
The ancient towers of Trim;
And County Meath and Dangan Hall
They did rewisit him.

I phansy of him so
His good old thoughts employin';
Fourscore years and one ago
Beside the flowin' Boyne.

His father praps he sees,
Most Musicle of Lords,
A playing maddrigles and glees
Upon the Arpsicords.

Jest phansy this old Ero
Upon his mother's knee!
Did ever lady in this land
Ave greater sons than she?

And I shoudn be surprize
While this was in his mind,
If a drop there twinkled in his eyes
Of unfamiliar brind.

To Hapsly Ouse next day
Drives up a Broosh and for,
A gracious prince sits in that Shay
(I mention him with Hor!)

They ring upon the bell,
The Porter shows his Ed,
(He fought at Vaterloo as vell,
And vears a Veskit red).

To see that carriage come,
The people round it press:
"And is the galliant Duke at ome?"
"Your Royal Ighness, yes."

He stepps from out the Broosh
And in the gate is gone;
And X, although the people push,
Says wary kind, "Move hon."

The Royal Prince unto
The galliant Duke did say,
"Dear duke, my little son and you
Was born the self same day.

"The Lady of the land,
My wife and Sovring dear,
It is by her horgust command
I wait upon you here.

"That lady is as well
As can expected be;

And to your Grace she bid me tell
This gracious message free.

"That offspring of our race,
Whom yesterday you see,
To show our honor for your Grace,
Prince Arthur he shall be.

"That name it rhymes to fame;
All Europe knows the sound:
And I couldn't find a better name
If you'd give me twenty pound.

"King Arthur had his knights
That girt his table round,
But you have won a hundred fights,
Will match 'em I'll be bound.

"You fought with Bonypart,
And likewise Tippoo Saib;
I name you then with all my heart
The Godsire of this babe."

That Prince his leave was took,
His hinterview was done.
So let us give the good old Duke
Good luck of his god-son.

And wish him years of joy
In this our time of Schism,
And hope he'll hear the royal boy
His little catechism.

And my pooty little Prince
That's come our arts to cheer,
Let me my loyal powers ewince
A welcomin of you ere.

And the Poit-Laureat's crownd,
I think, in some respex,
Egstremely shootable might be found
For honest Pleaseman X.

* The birth of Prince Arthur.

Galliant gents and lovely ladies,
List a tail vich late befel,
Vich I heard it, bein on duty,
At the Pleace Hoffice, Clerkenwell.

Praps you know the Fondling Chapel,
Vere the little children sings:
(Lor! I likes to hear on Sundies
Them there pooty little things!)

In this street there lived a housemaid,
If you particklarly ask me where—
Vy, it vas at four-and-tventy
Guilford Street, by Brunsvick Square.

Vich her name was Eliza Davis,
And she went to fetch the beer:
In the street she met a party
As was quite surprized to see her.

Vich he vas a British Sailor,
For to judge him by his look:
Tarry jacket, canvass trowsies,
Ha-la Mr. T. P. Cooke.

Presently this Mann accostes
Of this hinnocent young gal—
"Pray," saysee, "excuse my freedom,
You're so like my Sister Sal!

"You're so like my Sister Sally,
Both in valk and face and size,
Miss, that—dang my old lee scuppers,
It brings tears into my heyes!"

"I'm a mate on board a wessel,
I'm a sailor bold and true;
Shiver up my poor old timbers,
Let me be a mate for you!

"What's your name, my beauty, tell me;"
And she faintly hansers, "Lore,
Sir, my name's Eliza Davis,
And I live at tventy-four."

Hoftimes came this British seaman,
This deluded gal to meet;

And at tventy-four was welcome,
Tventy-four in Guilford Street.

And Eliza told her Master
(Kinder they than Missuses are),
How in marridge he had ast her,
Like a galliant Brittish Tar.

And he brought his landlady vith him,
(Vich vas all his hartful plan),
And she told how Charley Thompson
Reely vas a good young man.

And how she herself had lived in
Many years of union sweet,
Vith a gent she met promiskous,
Valkin in the public street.

And Eliza listened to them,
And she thought that soon their bands
Vould be published at the Fondlin,
Hand the clergymen jine their ands.

And he ast about the lodgers,
(Vich her master let some rooms),
Likevise vere they kep their things, and
Vere her master kep his spoons.

Hand this vicked Charley Thompson
Came on Sundy veek to see her;
And he sent Eliza Davis
Hout to fetch a pint of beer.

Hand while pore Eliza vent to
Fetch the beer, dewoid of sin,
This etrocious Charley Thompson
Let his wile accomplish him.

To the lodgers, their apartments,
This abandingd female goes,
Prigs their shirts and umberellas;
Prigs their boots, and hats, and clothes.

Vile the scoundrel Charley Thompson,
Lest his wictim should escape,
Hocust her vith rum and vater,
Like a fiend in huming shape.

But a hi was fixt upon 'em
Vich these raskles little sore;
Namely, Mr. Hide, the landlord
Of the house at tventy-four.

He vas valkin in his garden,
Just afore he vent to sup;
And on looking up he sor the
Lodgers' vinders lighted hup.

Hup the stairs the landlord tumbled;
Something's going wrong, he said;
And he caught the vicked voman
Underneath the lodgers' bed.

And he called a brother Pleaseman,
Vich vas passing on his beat;
Like a true and galliant feller,
Hup and down in Guilford Street.

And that Pleaseman able-bodied
Took this voman to the cell;
To the cell vere she was quodded,
In the Close of Clerkenwell.

And though vicked Charley Thompson
Boulted like a miscrant base,
Presently another Pleaseman
Took him to the self-same place.

And this precious pair of raskles
Tuesday last came up for doom;
By the beak they was committed,
Vich his name was Mr. Combe.

Has for poor Eliza Davis,
Simple gurl of tventy-four,
SHE I ope, vill never listen
In the streets to sailors moar.

But if she must ave a sweet-art,
(Vich most every gurl expex,)
Let her take a jolly pleaseman;
Vich his name peraps is—X.

DAMAGES, TWO HUNDRED POUNDS

Special Jurymen of England! who admire your country's laws,
And proclaim a British Jury worthy of the realm's applause;
Gayly compliment each other at the issue of a cause
Which was tried at Guildford 'sizes, this day week as ever was.

Unto that august tribunal comes a gentleman in grief,
(Special was the British Jury, and the Judge, the Baron Chief,)
Comes a British man and husband—asking of the law relief;
For his wife was stolen from him—he'd have vengeance on the thief.

Yes, his wife, the blessed treasure with the which his life was crowned,
Wickedly was ravished from him by a hypocrite profound.
And he comes before twelve Britons, men for sense and truth renowned,
To award him for his damage, twenty hundred sterling pound.

He by counsel and attorney there at Guildford does appear,
Asking damage of the villain who seduced his lady dear:
But I can't help asking, though the lady's guilt was all too clear,
And though guilty the defendant, wasn't the plaintiff rather queer?

First the lady's mother spoke, and said she'd seen her daughter cry
But a fortnight after marriage: early times for piping eye.
Six months after, things were worse, and the piping eye was black,
And this gallant British husband caned his wife upon the back.

Three months after they were married, husband pushed her to the door,
Told her to be off and leave him, for he wanted her no more.
As she would not go, why HE went: thrice he left his lady dear;
Left her, too, without a penny, for more than a quarter of a year.

Mrs. Frances Duncan knew the parties very well indeed,
She had seen him pull his lady's nose and make her lip to bleed;
If he chanced to sit at home not a single word he said:
Once she saw him throw the cover of a dish at his lady's head.

Sarah Green, another witness, clear did to the jury note
How she saw this honest fellow seize his lady by the throat,
How he cursed her and abused her, beating her into a fit,
Till the pitying next-door neighbors crossed the wall and witnessed it.

Next door to this injured Briton Mr. Owers a butcher dwelt;
Mrs. Owers's foolish heart towards this erring dame did melt;
(Not that she had erred as yet, crime was not developed in her),
But being left without a penny, Mrs. Owers supplied her dinner—
God be merciful to Mrs. Owers, who was merciful to this sinner!

Caroline Naylor was their servant, said they led a wretched life,

Saw this most distinguished Briton fling a teacup at his wife;
He went out to balls and pleasures, and never once, in ten months' space,
Sat with his wife or spoke her kindly. This was the defendant's case.

Pollock, C.B., charged the Jury; said the woman's guilt was clear:
That was not the point, however, which the Jury came to hear;
But the damage to determine which, as it should true appear,
This most tender-hearted husband, who so used his lady dear—

Beat her, kicked her, caned her, cursed her, left her starving, year by year,
Flung her from him, parted from her, wrung her neck, and boxed her ear—
What the reasonable damage this afflicted man could claim,
By the loss of the affections of this guilty graceless dame?

Then the honest British Twelve, to each other turning round,
Laid their clever heads together with a wisdom most profound:
And towards his Lordship looking, spoke the foreman wise and sound;—
"My Lord, we find for this here plaintiff, damages two hundred pound."

So, God bless the Special Jury! pride and joy of English ground,
And the happy land of England, where true justice does abound!
British jurymen and husbands, let us hail this verdict proper:
If a British wife offends you, Britons, you've a right to whop her.

Though you promised to protect her, though you promised to defend her,
You are welcome to neglect her: to the devil you may send her:
You may strike her, curse, abuse her; so declares our law renowned;
And if after this you lose her,—why, you're paid two hundred pound.

THE KNIGHT AND THE LADY

There's in the Vest a city pleasant
To vich King Bladud gev his name,
And in that city there's a Crescent
Vere dwelt a noble knight of fame.

Although that galliant knight is oldish,
Although Sir John as gray, gray air,
Hage has not made his busum coldish,
His Art still beats tewodds the Fair!

'Twas two years sins, this knight so splendid,
Peraps fateagued with Bath's routines,
To Paris towne his phootsteps bended
In sutch of gayer folks and seans.

His and was free, his means was easy,
A nobler, finer gent than he
Ne'er drove about the Shons-Eleesy,
Or paced the Roo de Rivolee.

A brougham and pair Sir John prowided,
In which abroad he loved to ride;
But ar! he most of all enjyed it,
When some one helse was sittin' inside!

That "some one helse" a lovely dame was
Dear ladies you will heasy tell—
Countess Grabrowski her sweet name was,
A noble title, ard to spell.

This faymus Countess ad a daughter
Of lovely form and tender art;
A nobleman in marridge sought her,
By name the Baron of Saint Bart.

Their pashn touched the noble Sir John,
It was so pewer and profound;
Lady Grabrowski he did urge on
With Hyming's wreeth their loves to crownd.

"O, come to Bath, to Lansdowne Crescent,"
Says kind Sir John, "and live with me;
The living there's uncommon pleasant—
I'm sure you'll find the hair agree.

"O, come to Bath, my fair Grabrowski,
And bring your charming girl," sezee;
"The Barring here shall have the ouse-key,
Vith breakfast, dinner, lunch, and tea.

"And when they've passed an appy winter,
Their opes and loves no more we'll bar;
The marridge-vow they'll enter inter,
And I at church will be their Par."

To Bath they went to Lansdowne Crescent,
Where good Sir John he did provide
No end of teas and balls incessant,
And hosses both to drive and ride.

He was so Ospitably busy,
When Miss was late, he'd make so bold
Upstairs to call out, "Missy, Missy,

Come down, the coffy's getting cold!"

But O! 'tis sadd to think such bounties
Should meet with such return as this;
O Barring of Saint Bart, O Countess
Grabrowski, and O cruel Miss!

He married you at Bath's fair Habby,
Saint Bart he treated like a son—
And wasn't it uncommon shabby
To do what you have went and done!

My trembling And amost refewses
To write the charge which Sir John swore,
Of which the Countess he ecuses,
Her daughter and her son-in-lore.

My Mews quite blushes as she sings of
The fatle charge which now I quote:
He says Miss took his two best rings off,
And pawned 'em for a tenpun note.

"Is this the child of honest parince,
To make away with folks' best things?
Is this, pray, like the wives of Barrins,
To go and prig a gentleman's rings?"

Thus thought Sir John, by anger wrought on,
And to rewenge his injured cause,
He brought them hup to Mr. Broughton,
Last Vensday veek as ever waws.

If guiltless, how she have been slandered!
If guilty, wengeance will not fail:
Meanwhile the lady is remanded
And gev three hundred pouns in bail.

JACOB HOMNIUM'S HOSS

A NEW PALLICE COURT CHANT

One sees in Viteall Yard,
Vere pleacemen do resort,
A wenerable hinstitute,
'Tis call'd the Pallis Court.
A gent as got his i on it,

I think 'twill make some sport.

The natur of this Court
My hindignation riles:
A few fat legal spiders
Here set & spin their viles;
To rob the town theyr privlege is,
In a hayrea of twelve miles.

The Judge of this year Court
Is a mellitary beak,
He knows no more of Lor
Than praps he does of Greek,
And prowides hisself a deputy
Because he cannot speak.

Four counsel in this Court—
Misnamed of Justice—sits;
These lawyers owes their places to
Their money, not their wits;
And there's six attornies under them,
As here their living gits.

These lawyers, six and four,
Was a livin at their ease,
A sendin of their writs abowt,
And droring in the fees,
When their erose a cirkimstance
As is like to make a breeze.

It now is some monce since,
A gent both good and trew
Possest an ansum oss vith vich
He didn know what to do:
Peraps he did not like the oss;
Peraps he was a scru.

This gentleman his oss
At Tattersall's did lodge;
There came a wulgar oss-dealer,
This gentleman's name did fodge,
And took the oss from Tattersall's
Wasn that a artful dodge?

One day this gentleman's groom
This willain did spy out,
A mounted on this oss
A ridin him about;

"Get out of that there oss, you rogue,"
Speaks up the groom so stout.

The thief was cruel whex'd
To find himself so pinn'd;
The oss began to whinny,
The honest gloom he grinn'd;
And the raskle thief got off the oss
And cut avay like vind.

And phansy with what joy
The master did regard
His dearly bluvd lost oss again
Trot in the stable yard!

Who was this master good
Of whomb I makes these rhymes?
His name is Jacob Homnium, Exquire;
And if I'd committed crimes,
Good Lord I wouldn't ave that mann
Attack me in the Times!

Now shortly after the groomb
His master's oss did take up,
There came a livery-man
This gentleman to wake up;
And he handed in a little bill,
Which hangered Mr. Jacob.

For two pound seventeen
This livery-man eplied,
For the keep of Mr. Jacob's oss,
Which the thief had took to ride.
"Do you see anythink green in me?"
Mr. Jacob Homnium cried.

"Because a raskle chews
My oss away to robb,
And goes tick at your Mews
For seven-and-fifty bobb,
Shall I be call'd to pay?—It is
A iniquitious Jobb."

Thus Mr. Jacob cut
The conwasation short;
The livery-man went ome,
Detummingd to ave sport,
And summingsd Jacob Homnium, Exquire,

Into the Pallis Court.

Pore Jacob went to Court,
A Counsel for to fix,
And choose a barrister out of the four,
An attorney of the six:
And there he sor these men of Lor,
And watch'd 'em at their tricks.

The dreadful day of trile
In the Pallis Court did come;
The lawyers said their say,
The Judge look'd wery glum,
And then the British Jury cast
Pore Jacob Hom-ni-um.

O a weary day was that
For Jacob to go through;
The debt was two seventeen
(Which he no mor owed than you),
And then there was the plaintives costs,
Eleven pound six and two.

And then there was his own,
Which the lawyers they did fix
At the wery moderit figgar
Of ten pound one and six.
Now Evins bless the Pallis Court,
And all its bold ver-dicks!

I cannot settingly tell
If Jacob swaw and cust,
At aving for to pay this sumb;
But I should think he must,
And av drawn a cheque for L24 4s. 8d.
With most igstreme disgust.

O Pallis Court, you move
My pitty most profound.
A most emusing sport
You thought it, I'll be bound,
To saddle hup a three-pound debt,
With two-and-twenty pound.

Good sport it is to you
To grind the honest pore,
To pay their just or unjust debts
With eight hundred per cent. for Lor;

Make haste and get your costes in,
They will not last much mor!

Come down from that tribewn,
Thou shameless and Unjust;
Thou Swindle, picking pockets in
The name of Truth august:
Come down, thou hoary blasphemy,
For die thou shalt and must.

And go it, Jacob Homnium,
And ply your iron pen,
And rise up, Sir John Jervis,
And shut me up that den;
That sty for fattening lawyers in,
On the bones of honest men.

PLEACEMAN X.

THE SPECULATORS

The night was stormy and dark,
The town was shut up in sleep:
Only those were abroad who were out on a lark,
Or those who'd no beds to keep.

I pass'd through the lonely street,
The wind did sing and blow;
I could hear the policeman's feet
Clapping to and fro.

There stood a potato-man
In the midst of all the wet;
He stood with his 'tato-can
In the lonely Hay-market.

Two gents of dismal mien,
And dank and greasy rags,
Came out of a shop for gin,
Swaggering over the flags:

Swaggering over the stones,
These shabby bucks did walk;
And I went and followed those seedy ones,
And listened to their talk.

Was I sober or awake?
Could I believe my ears?
Those dismal beggars spake
Of nothing but railroad shares.

I wondered more and more:
Says one—"Good friend of mine,
How many shares have you wrote for,
In the Diddlesex Junction line?"

"I wrote for twenty," says Jim,
"But they wouldn't give me one;"
His comrade straight rebuked him
For the folly he had done:

"O Jim, you are unawares
Of the ways of this bad town;
I always write for five hundred shares,
And THEN they put me down."

"And yet you got no shares,"
Says Jim, "for all your boast;"
"I WOULD have wrote," says Jack, "but where
Was the penny to pay the post?"

"I lost, for I couldn't pay
That first instalment up;
But here's 'taters smoking hot—I say,
Let's stop, my boy, and sup."

And at this simple feast
The while they did regale,
I drew each ragged capitalist
Down on my left thumbnail.

Their talk did me perplex,
All night I tumbled and tost,
And thought of railroad specs,
And how money was won and lost.

"Bless railroads everywhere,"
I said, "and the world's advance;
Bless every railroad share
In Italy, Ireland, France;
For never a beggar need now despair,
And every rogue has a chance."

OF THE PROTESTANT CONSPIRACY TO TAKE THE POPE'S LIFE.

(BY A GENTLEMAN WHO HAS BEEN ON THE SPOT.)

Come all ye Christian people, unto my tale give ear,
'Tis about a base consperracy, as quickly shall appear;
'Twill make your hair to bristle up, and your eyes to start and glow,
When of this dread consperracy you honest folks shall know.

The news of this consperracy and villianous attempt,
I read it in a newspaper, from Italy it was sent:
It was sent from lovely Italy, where the olives they do grow,
And our holy father lives, yes, yes, while his name it is No NO.

And 'tis there our English noblemen goes that is Puseyites no longer,
Because they finds the ancient faith both better is and stronger,
And 'tis there I knelt beside my lord when he kiss'd the POPE his toe,
And hung his neck with chains at St. Peter's Vinculo.

And 'tis there the splendid churches is, and the fountains playing grand,
And the palace of PRINCE TORLONIA, likewise the Vatican;
And there's the stairs where the bagpipe-men and the piffararys blow.
And it's there I drove my lady and lord in the Park of Pincio.

And 'tis there our splendid churches is in all their pride and glory,
Saint Peter's famous Basilisk and Saint Mary's Maggiory;
And them benighted Prodestants, on Sunday they must go
Outside the town to the preaching-shop by the gate of Popolo.

Now in this town of famous Room, as I dessay you have heard,
There is scarcely any gentleman as hasn't got a beard.
And ever since the world began it was ordained so,
That there should always barbers be wheresumever beards do grow.

And as it always has been so since the world it did begin,
The POPE, our Holy Potentate, has a beard upon his chin;
And every morning regular when cocks begin to crow,
There comes a certing party to wait on POPE PIO.

There comes a certing gintlemen with razier, soap, and lather,
A shaving most respectfully the POPE, our Holy Father.
And now the dread consperracy I'll quickly to you show,
Which them sanguinary Prodestants did form against NONO.

Them sanguinary Prodestants, which I abore and hate,
Assembled in the preaching-shop by the Flaminian gate;
And they took counsel with their selves to deal a deadly blow
Against our gentle Father, the Holy POPE PIO.

Exhibiting a wickedness which I never heard or read of;
What do you think them Prodestants wished? to cut the good Pope's head off!
And to the kind POPE'S Air-dresser the Prodestant Clark did go,
And proposed him to decapitate the innocent PIO.

"What hever can be easier," said this Clerk—this Man of Sin,
"When you are called to hoperate on His Holiness's chin,
Than just to give the razier a little slip—just so?—
And there's an end, dear barber, of innocent PIO!"

The wicked conversation it chanced was overerd
By an Italian lady; she heard it every word:
Which by birth she was a Marchioness, in service forced to go
With the parson of the preaching-shop at the gate of Popolo.

When the lady heard the news, as duty did obleege,
As fast as her legs could carry her she ran to the Poleege.
"O Polegia," says she (for they pronounts it so),
"They're going for to massyker our Holy POPE PIO.

"The ebomminable Englishmen, the Parsing and his Clark,
His Holiness's Air-dresser devised it in the dark!
And I would recommend you in prison for to throw
These villians would esassinate the Holy POPE PIO?

"And for saving of His Holiness and his trebble crownd
I humbly hope your Worships will give me a few pound;
Because I was a Marchioness many years ago,
Before I came to service at the gate of Popolo."

That sackreligious Air-dresser, the Parson and his man
Wouldn't, though ask'd continyally, own their wicked plan—
And so the kind Authoraties let those villians go
That was plotting of the murder of the good PIO NONO.

Now isn't this safishnt proof, ye gentlemen at home,
How wicked is them Prodestants, and how good our Pope at Rome?
So let us drink confusion to LORD JOHN and LORD MINTO,
And a health unto His Eminence, and good PIO NONO.

THE LAMENTABLE BALLAD OF THE FOUNDLING OF SHOREDITCH

Come all ye Christian people, and listen to my tail,
It is all about a doctor was travelling by the rail,
By the Heastern Counties' Railway (vich the shares I don't desire),
From Ixworth town in Suffolk, vich his name did not transpire.

A travelling from Bury this Doctor was employed
With a gentleman, a friend of his, vich his name was Captain Loyd,
And on reaching Marks Tey Station, that is next beyond Colchester,
A lady entered into them most elegantly dressed.

She entered into the Carriage all with a tottering step,
And a pooty little Bayby upon her bussum slep;
The gentlemen received her with kindness and siwillaty,
Pitying this lady for her illness and debillaty.

She had a fust-class ticket, this lovely lady said,
Because it was so lonesome she took a secknd instead.
Better to travel by secknd class, than sit alone in the fust,
And the pooty little Baby upon her breast she nust.

A seein of her cryin, and shiverin and pail,
To her spoke this surging, the Ero of my tail;
Saysee you look unwell, Ma'am, I'll elp you if I can,
And you may tell your ease to me, for I'm a meddicle man.

"Thank you, Sir," the lady said, "I only look so pale,
Because I ain't accustom'd to travelling on the Rale;
I shall be better presnly, when I've ad some rest:"
And that pooty little Baby she squeeged it to her breast.

So in the conwersation the journey they beguiled,
Capting Loyd and the meddicle man, and the lady and the child,
Till the warious stations along the line was passed,
For even the Heastern Counties' trains must come in at last.

When at Shoreditch tumminus at lenth stopped the train,
This kind meddicle gentleman proposed his aid again.
"Thank you, Sir," the lady said, "for your kyindness dear;
My carridge and my osses is probibbly come here.

"Will you old this baby, please, vilst I step and see?"
The Doctor was a famly man: "That I will," says he.
Then the little child she kist, kist it very gently,
Vich was sucking his little fist, sleeping innocently.

With a sigh from her art, as though she would have bust it,
Then she gave the Doctor the child—wery kind he nust it:

Hup then the lady jumped hoff the bench she sat from,
Tumbled down the carridge steps and ran along the platform.

Vile hall the other passengers vent upon their vays,
The Capting and the Doctor sat there in a maze;
Some vent in a Homminibus, some vent in a Cabby,
The Capting and the Doctor vaited vith the babby.

There they sat looking queer, for an hour or more,
But their feller passinger neather on 'em sore:
Never, never back again did that lady come
To that pooty sleeping Hinfnt a suckin of his Thum!

What could this pore Doctor do, bein treated thus,
When the darling Baby woke, cryin for its nuss?
Off he drove to a female friend, vich she was both kind and mild,
And igsplained to her the circumstance of this year little child.

That kind lady took the child instantly in her lap,
And made it very comfortable by giving it some pap;
And when she took its close off, what d'you think she found?
A couple of ten pun notes sewn up, in its little gownd!

Also in its little close, was a note which did conwey
That this little baby's parents lived in a handsome way
And for his Headucation they reglarly would pay,
And sirtingly like gentlefolks would claim the child one day,
If the Christian people who'd charge of it would say,
Per adwertisement in The Times where the baby lay.

Pity of this bayy many people took,
It had such pooty ways and such a pooty look;
And there came a lady forrard (I wish that I could see
Any kind lady as would do as much for me);

And I wish with all my art, some night in MY night gownd,
I could find a note stitched for ten or twenty pound—
There came a lady forrard, that most honorable did say,
She'd adopt this little baby, which her parents cast away.

While the Doctor pondered on this hoffer fair,
Comes a letter from Devonshire, from a party there,
Hordering the Doctor, at its Mar's desire,
To send the little Infant back to Devonshire.

Lost in apoplexity, this pore meddicle man,
Like a sensable gentleman, to the Justice ran;
Which his name was Mr. Hammill, a honorable beak,

That takes his seat in Worship Street, four times a week.

"O Justice!" says the Doctor, "instrugt me what to do.
I've come up from the country, to throw myself on you;
My patients have no doctor to tend them in their ills,
(There they are in Suffolk without their drafts and pills!)

"I've come up from the country, to know how I'll dispose
Of this pore little baby, and the twenty pun note, and the close,
And I want to go back to Suffolk, dear Justice, if you please,
And my patients wants their Doctor, and their Doctor wants his feez."

Up spoke Mr. Hammill, sittin at his desk,
"This year application does me much perplesk;
What I do adwise you, is to leave this babby
In the Parish where it was left, by its mother shabby."

The Doctor from his worship sadly did depart—
He might have left the baby, but he hadn't got the heart
To go for to leave that Hinnocent, has the law allows,
To the tender mussies of the Union House.

Mother, who left this little one on a stranger's knee,
Think how cruel you have been, and how good was he!
Think, if you've been guilty, innocent was she;
And do not take unkindly this little word of me:
Heaven be merciful to us all, sinners as we be!

THE ORGAN-BOY'S APPEAL

"WESTMINSTER POLICE COURT.—Policeman X brought a paper of doggerel verses to the MAGISTRATE, which had been thrust into his hands, X said, by an Italian boy, who ran away immediately afterwards.

"The MAGISTRATE, after perusing the lines, looked hard at X, and said he did not think they were written by an Italian.

"X, blushing, said he thought the paper read in Court last week, and which frightened so the old gentleman to whom it was addressed, was also not of Italian origin."

O SIGNOR BRODERIP, you are a wickid ole man,
You wexis us little horgin-boys whenever you can:
How dare you talk of Justice, and go for to seek
To pussicute us horgin-boys, you senguinary Beek?

Though you set in Vestminster surrounded by your crushers,
Harrogint and habsolute like the Hortocrat of hall the Rushers,

Yet there is a better vurld I'd have you for to know,
Likewise a place vere the henimies of horgin-boys will go.

O you vickid HEROD without any pity!
London vithout horgin-boys vood be a dismal city.
Sweet SAINT CICILY who first taught horgin-pipes to blow,
Soften the heart of this Magistrit that haggerywates us so!

Good Italian gentlemen, fatherly and kind,
Brings us over to London here our horgins for to grind;
Sends us out vith little vite mice and guinea-pigs also
A popping of the Veasel and a Jumpin of JIM CROW.

And as us young horgin-boys is grateful in our turn
We gives to these kind gentlemen hall the money we earn,
Because that they vood vop up as wery wel we know
Unless we brought our hurnings back to them as loves us so.

O MR. BRODERIP! wery much I'm surprise,
Ven you take your valks abroad where can be your eyes?
If a Beak had a heart then you'd compryend
Us pore little horgin-boys was the poor man's friend.

Don't you see the shildren in the droring-rooms
Clapping of their little ands when they year our toons?
On their mothers' bussums don't you see the babbies crow
And down to us dear horgin-boys lots of apence throw?

Don't you see the ousemaids (pooty POLLIES and MARIES),
Ven ve bring our urdigurdis, smiling from the hairies?
Then they come out vith a slice o' cole puddn or a bit o' bacon or so
And give it us young horgin-boys for lunch afore we go.

Have you ever seen the Hirish children sport
When our velcome music-box brings sunshine in the Court?
To these little paupers who can never pay
Surely all good horgin-boys, for GOD'S love, will play.

Has for those proud gentlemen, like a serting B—k
(Vich I von't be pussonal and therefore vil not speak),
That flings their parler-vinders hup von ve begin to play
And cusses us and swears at us in such a wiolent way,

Instedd of their abewsing and calling hout Poleece
Let em send out JOHN to us with six-pence or a shillin apiece.
Then like good young horgin-boys avay from there we'll go,
Blessing sweet SAINT CICILY that taught our pipes to blow.

LITTLE BILLEE.*

Air—"Il y avait un petit navire."
There were three sailors of Bristol city
Who took a boat and went to sea.
But first with beef and captain's biscuits
And pickled pork they loaded she.

There was gorging Jack and guzzling Jimmy,
And the youngest he was little Billee.
Now when they got as far as the Equator
They'd nothing left but one split pea.

Says gorging Jack to guzzling Jimmy,
"I am extremely hungaree."
To gorging Jack says guzzling Jimmy,
"We've nothing left, us must eat we."

Says gorging Jack to guzzling Jimmy,
"With one another we shouldn't agree!
There's little Bill, he's young and tender,
We're old and tough, so let's eat he.

"Oh! Billy, we're going to kill and eat you,
So undo the button of your chemie."
When Bill received this information
He used his pocket handkerchie.

"First let me say my catechism,
Which my poor mamy taught to me."
"Make haste, make haste," says guzzling Jimmy,
While Jack pulled out his snickersnee.

So Billy went up to the main-top gallant mast,
And down he fell on his bended knee.
He scarce had come to the twelfth commandment
When up he jumps. "There's land I see:

"Jerusalem and Madagascar,
And North and South Amerikee:
There's the British flag a riding at anchor,
With Admiral Napier, K.C.B."

So when they got aboard of the Admiral's
He hanged fat Jack and flogged Jimmee;
But as for little Bill he made him

The Captain of a Seventy-three.

As different versions of this popular song have been set to music and sung, no apology is needed for the insertion in these pages of what is considered to be the correct version.

The play is done; the curtain drops,
Slow falling to the prompter's bell:
A moment yet the actor stops,
And looks around, to say farewell.
It is an irksome word and task;
And, when he's laughed and said his say,
He shows, as he removes the mask,
A face that's anything but gay.

One word, ere yet the evening ends,
Let's close it with a parting rhyme,
And pledge a hand to all young friends,
As fits the merry Christmas time.
On life's wide scene you, too, have parts,
That Fate ere long shall bid you play;
Good night! with honest gentle hearts
A kindly greeting go alway!

Goodnight—I'd say, the griefs, the joys,
Just hinted in this mimic page,
The triumphs and defeats of boys,
Are but repeated in our age.
I'd say, your woes were not less keen,
Your hopes more vain than those of men;
Your pangs or pleasures of fifteen
At forty-five played o'er again.

I'd say, we suffer and we strive,
Not less nor more as men, than boys;
With grizzled beards at forty-five,
As erst at twelve in corduroys.
And if, in time of sacred youth,
We learned at home to love and pray,
Pray Heaven that early Love and Truth
May never wholly pass away.

And in the world, as in the school,
I'd say, how fate may change and shift;
The prize be sometimes with the fool,

The race not always to the swift.
The strong may yield, the good may fall,
The great man be a vulgar clown,
The knave be lifted over all,
The kind cast pitilessly down.

Who knows the inscrutable design?
Blessed be He who took and gave!
Why should your mother, Charles, not mine,
Be weeping at her darling's grave?
We bow to Heaven that will'd it so,
That darkly rules the fate of all,
That sends the respite or the blow,
That's free to give, or to recall.

This crowns his feast with wine and wit:
Who brought him to that mirth and state?
His betters, see, below him sit,
Or hunger hopeless at the gate.
Who bade the mud from Dives' wheel
To spurn the rags of Lazarus?
Come, brother, in that dust we'll kneel,
Confessing Heaven that ruled it thus.

So each shall mourn, in life's advance,
Dear hopes, dear friends, untimely killed;
Shall grieve for many a forfeit chance,
And longing passion unfulfilled.
Amen! whatever fate be sent,
Pray God the heart may kindly glow,
Although the head with cares be bent,
And whitened with the winter snow.

Come wealth or want, come good or ill,
Let young and old accept their part,
And bow before the Awful Will,
And bear it with an honest heart,
Who misses or who wins the prize.
Go, lose or conquer as you can;
But if you fail, or if you rise,
Be each, pray God, a gentleman.

A gentleman, or old or young!
(Bear kindly with my humble lays);
The sacred chorus first was sung
Upon the first of Christmas days:
The shepherds heard it overhead—
The joyful angels raised it then:

Glory to Heaven on high, it said,
And peace on earth to gentle men.

My song, save this, is little worth;
I lay the weary pen aside,
And wish you health, and love, and mirth,
As fits the solemn Christmas-tide.
As fits the holy Christmas birth,
Be this, good friends, our carol still—
Be peace on earth, be peace on earth,
To men of gentle will.

VANITAS VANITATUM

How spake of old the Royal Seer?
(His text is one I love to treat on.)
This life of ours he said is sheer
Mataiotes Mataioteton.

O Student of this gilded Book,
Declare, while musing on its pages,
If truer words were ever spoke
By ancient, or by modern sages!

The various authors' names but note,*
French, Spanish, English, Russians, Germans:
And in the volume polyglot,
Sure you may read a hundred sermons!

What histories of life are here,
More wild than all romancers' stories;
What wondrous transformations queer,
What homilies on human glories!

What theme for sorrow or for scorn!
What chronicle of Fate's surprises—
Of adverse fortune nobly borne,
Of chances, changes, ruins, rises!

Of thrones upset, and sceptres broke,
How strange a record here is written!
Of honors, dealt as if in joke;
Of brave desert unkindly smitten.

How low men were, and how they rise!

How high they were, and how they tumble!
O vanity of vanities!
O laughable, pathetic jumble!

Here between honest Janin's joke
And his Turk Excellency's firman,
I write my name upon the book:
I write my name—and end my sermon.

O Vanity of vanities!
How wayward the decrees of Fate are;
How very weak the very wise,
How very small the very great are!

What mean these stale moralities,
Sir Preacher, from your desk you mumble?
Why rail against the great and wise,
And tire us with your ceaseless grumble?

Pray choose us out another text,
O man morose and narrow-minded!
Come turn the page—I read the next,
And then the next, and still I find it.

Read here how Wealth aside was thrust,
And Folly set in place exalted;
How Princes footed in the dust,
While lackeys in the saddle vaulted.

Though thrice a thousand years are past,
Since David's son, the sad and splendid,
The weary King Ecclesiast,
Upon his awful tablets penned it,—

Methinks the text is never stale,
And life is every day renewing
Fresh comments on the old old tale
Of Folly, Fortune, Glory, Ruin.

Hark to the Preacher, preaching still
He lifts his voice and cries his sermon,
Here at St. Peter's of Cornhill,
As yonder on the Mount of Hermon;

For you and me to heart to take
(O dear beloved brother readers)
To-day as when the good King spake
Beneath the solemn Syrian cedars.

William Makepeace Thackeray – A Short Biography

William Makepeace Thackeray, was born on July 18th, 1811 in Calcutta, then British India, where his father, Richmond Thackeray was the secretary to the Board of Revenue in the British East India Company. His mother, Anne Becher also worked for the British East India Company.

His father died in 1815, and his mother sent Thackeray to England the following year while she remained in India and would, sometime later, marry her childhood sweetheart. En-route to England the ship stopped for provisions on St. Helena. The Imprisoned Napoleon was pointed out to him by a servant with the words that he "eats three sheep every day, and all the little children he can lay hands on!"

Finally, back in England the young Thackeray was sent to school, initially in Southampton and Chiswick, before being moved to Charterhouse School. Charterhouse and Thackeray did not take to each other but the time became a valuable source for his later work "Slaughterhouse". Despite his less than respectful recalling of his time with them Charterhouse placed a monument in the chapel after his death.

In his final year at Charterhouse a troubling illness delayed his departure to attend Cambridge University. Over the course of his life Thackeray would suffer from ill health, much of it brought about for his fondness for "gluttling and gorging". Excess was something he could enjoy and for a man who stood some 6' 3" it would appear to the eye that, initially at least, his large frame could absorb much of that excess.

However, Thackeray's lazy attitude to completely mastering anything he set his mind too, especially where ambition for academia was involved, meant he departed Cambridge little more than a year after joining. He had however published two short works in University periodicals. As an author, he would have quite some impact on English literature in the years to come, so it seems difficult to reconcile that he felt no urgency to pursue writing at that time.

He now spent some time travelling across Europe stopping at both Paris, to study art, and to winter in Weimar. Back in London a final attempt was made on a professional career. This time studying law at Middle Temple. It lasted no more than a few months.

Now, having reached 21, he received his father's inheritance. It was a very substantial estate of 17,000 pounds, an enormous sum of money at the time. However, although Thackeray had youth he lacked a little in energy and certainly much financial experience. He funded not one but two newspapers, and neither was to prove successful. Gambling seemed enjoyable and certainly he had money to lose, which he did on a regular basis. Further investments in two soon-to-fail Indian banks quickly ensured little of his good fortune remained.

He now had to consider taking up yet another profession. Thackeray turned to art hoping that his studies in Paris would prove of benefit. Unfortunately, they did not. His ambivalent attitude continued until on August 20th, 1836 he married the 20-year-old, Isabella Gethin Shawe. It seemed to prove a turning point in many ways.

The marriage would produce three daughters; Anne Isabella in 1837, Jane, in 1838, who tragically died in infancy and Harriet Marian in 1840.

Now, as a husband and father, Thackeray seemed at last to understand his responsibilities to nurture and provide.

His early efforts at "writing for his life" were to establish his career as a foremost author. His main employment was with Fraser's Magazine, a sharp-witted and sharp-tongued conservative publication for which he produced art criticism, short fictional sketches, and who would also serialise two of his novels. He also found time, between 1837 and 1840 to review books for The Times and to make regular contributions to The Morning Chronicle and The Foreign Quarterly Review.

In his earliest works, which he wrote under various pseudonyms including; Charles James Yellowplush, Michael Angelo Titmarsh and George Savage Fitz-Boodle, he tended towards savagery in his attacks on high society, military prowess, the institution of marriage and hypocrisy.

Between May 1839 and February 1840 Fraser's published Catherine. Originally intended as a satire of the Newgate school of crime fiction, it ended up being more of a picaresque tale. Thackeray also began work on what would eventually become A Shabby Genteel Story.

However, Thackeray, having successfully found a career that he cared about and had the talent for, found that his personal life was about to descend into chaos. After the birth of her third child in 1840, Isabella, sank into depression. At first Thackeray, didn't think too much of it. He needed to work to earn an income to support his family and finding that Isabella was distracting both herself and him he realised he could get no work done at home and so spent more and more time away until finally, in September 1840, it dawned upon him how serious his wife's condition had become. Struck by guilt, he set out with his wife to Ireland. During the boat crossing she threw herself into the sea, but was thankfully pulled from the waters. Her mother who had little understanding of her daughter's illness was of little help and perhaps a hinderance. After four-weeks they returned to England. From November 1840 to February 1842 Isabella was in and out of professional care, as her condition waxed and waned.

Isabella eventually deteriorated into a permanent state of detachment. Thackeray desperately sought cures for her, but nothing worked, and she ended up in two different asylums in or near Paris until 1845, after which Thackeray took her back to England, where he installed her with a Mrs Bakewell at Camberwell. Despite her condition Isabella would outlive her husband by 3 decades.

After his wife's illness Thackeray became a de facto widower, never able to establish another permanent relationship.

In 1843, through his connection to the illustrator John Leech, whom he had met at Charterhouse, he began writing for the newly created magazine Punch, in which he published The Snob Papers, later collected as The Book of Snobs. Thackeray was a regular contributor to Punch until 1854.

Thackeray had earlier received some success with two travel books, The Paris Sketch Book and The Irish Sketch Book, the latter marked by hostility to Irish Catholics. The book appealed to British prejudices, and on that basis Thackeray now became Punch's Irish expert, often under the pseudonym Hibernis Hibernior. It was Thackeray's writings that were the basis for Punch's notoriously harsh, hostile and condescending depictions of the Irish during the devastating Irish Famine (1845–51).

As well as his regular columns and contributions Thackeray worked on his novels. In The Luck of Barry Lyndon, which was serialised in Fraser's in 1844, he explored the situation of an outsider trying to achieve status in high society, a theme he developed more successfully a few years later with Vanity Fair.

Thackeray achieved more recognition with his Snob Papers (serialised 1846/7, and published as a book in 1848), but the work that really established his fame was the novel Vanity Fair, which first appeared in serialised instalments beginning in January 1847.

Published as a book the novel had a slow start but eventually sales rose to 7,000 copies a month. Just as importantly, it was the book that everybody was talking about. Thackeray finally had a name that gained notice and was reviewed in journals such as the famed, and much sought after, Edinburgh Review.

The accolades and success also gave him a respite from writing everything in a manner that would help ensure income rather than literary respect. Even before Vanity Fair completed its serial run Thackeray had become a celebrity, sought after by the very lords and ladies whom he satirised. with the character of Becky Sharp, the artist's daughter who rises high by manipulating all around her.

Pendennis followed in 1849-50, but it was interrupted halfway through writing for 3 months by a severe illness. Some accounts say it was cholera. Pendennis is a semi-autobiographical bildungsroman that draws on, among other things, Thackeray's disappointments in college, his ambivalent relationship with his mother, and his insider's knowledge of the London publishing world.

This novel ran at the same time as Charles Dicken's David Copperfield, and their dual appearance brought about the first of many comparisons with Dickens. Thackeray, for his part, felt that he and Dickens were battling for supremacy, though he would never equal Dickens's popularity, except with the critics.

Interestingly the two were involved in a spat which became known as the "Garrick Club affair". Thackeray and Dickens had skirmished over the "Dignity of Literature" and had other slight disagreements but this literary quarrel caused a rift in their friendship that lasted almost until the end of Thackeray's life. The relationship was healed only in Thackeray's last months, through a surprise meeting and handshake on the steps of a London club. Thackeray had taken offense at some personal remarks in a column by Edmund Yates and demanded an apology, eventually taking the affair to the Garrick Club committee. Already upset with Thackeray for an indiscreet remark about his affair with Ellen Ternan, Dickens championed Yates, helping him to write letters both to Thackeray and, in his defense, to the club's committee. Despite the intervention of Dickens, Yates eventually lost the vote of the Club's members, but the quarrel was laid out for the public in journal articles and pamphlets. "What pains me most," Thackeray said at the time, "is that Dickens should have been his adviser, and next that I should have had to lay a heavy hand on a young man who, I take it, has been cruelly punished by the issue of the affair, and I believe is hardly aware of the nature of his own offence, and doesn't even now understand that a gentleman should resent the monstrous insult which he volunteered".

Aside from these quarrelsome, distracting literary disagreements and Isabella's on-going illness life was good for Thackeray. He was to remain as he put it "at the top of the tree," for the rest of his life. The works for which he is so well remembered; Vanity Fair and Barry Lyndon had established that but he continued to write and produce novels, stories, sketches and works profusely.

To remain at such a high level in both quality and quantity is somewhat surprising given the continuation and escalation of various illnesses which continued to haunt him.

With Isabella still unwell Thackeray did seek out other women, in particular Mrs Jane Brookfield. Despite his hopes, it always felt that he was pursuing her as she battled the problems of her own marriage and turned to Thackeray for comfort and support. A source for these relationships often came on the lecture tours of Great Britain and the United States which he now entertained. These tours gave the public a chance to see and hear their hero's and provided another valuable source of income for those invited to tour. Whilst in in New York he met the Baxter family. Sally, the eldest daughter, enchanted the novelist—as a number of vibrant, intelligent, beautiful young women had done before her—and she became the model for Ethel Newcome. He visited her on his second tour of the States when she was married to a South Carolina gentleman. His choosing of married women in the shape of both Jane and Sally was ill-advised and both relationships led nowhere but did take quite some time to disassemble and for reason to set in.

In 1852, The History of Henry Esmond was published as a 3-volume novel without first being serialised and in a special type meant to imitate the appearance of an eighteenth-century book. This was the most carefully planned of Thackeray's novels. The book was celebrated for its brilliance, and Thackeray recognized it as "the very best I can do". At the time, it caused a sensation thanks to its controversial ending, wherein the hero marries a woman who early in the novel seemed more like a "mother" to him.

The eighteenth-century held a great attraction for Thackeray and he had previously set both Barry Lyndon and Catherine there as well as the sequel to Esmond, The Virginians, which takes place in North America and includes George Washington as a character.

Thackeray had twice visited the United States on lecture tours during this period as well as given lectures in London on the English humorists of the eighteenth century, and on the first four Hanoverian monarchs. The latter were published in a book as The Four Georges.

Interestingly Thackeray also decided that Politics was something he could more than dabble in. In Oxford he stood as an independent for Parliament. He was narrowly beaten by Cardwell, a politician who was substituted for the man Thackeray thought he was going to run against, although Thackeray's advocacy of entertainment on the Sabbath would have done little to help his campaign. Even so the margin of his defeat was only 1,070 votes, to Thackeray's 1,005.

In 1860 Thackeray became editor of the newly established Cornhill Magazine, a role he never felt truly comfortable in, preferring to contribute as a columnist on the Roundabout Papers. However, the financial compensation was by all accounts quite extraordinary. The Cornhill began its history with a record circulation and a number of distinguished contributors swayed onboard by Thackeray's reputation. It was in the Cornhill that he serialised his last complete novel, The Adventures of Philip in 1861-62. (After his death, the incomplete Denis Duval would also appear there in 1864).

After two years as editor he stepped down, primarily to concentrate on writing novels again. A piece he wrote for the Cornhill at this time "Thorns in the Cushion," one of The Roundabout Papers, fondly assembles the pains he felt in rejecting manuscripts on the one hand and receiving criticism of the magazine on the other. It seemed a good time to move on.

Thackeray's health had worsened during the 1850s and he was plagued by a recurring stricture of the urethra that laid him up for days at a time. He also felt that he had lost much of his creative impetus. He worsened matters by excessively eating and drinking, and avoiding exercise, though he enjoyed horseback-riding. He has been described as "the greatest literary glutton who ever lived". Indeed, his main activity apart from writing was eating and drinking and many of his stories include elaborate scenes and themes on his fondness for them.

On December 23rd, 1863, William Makepeace Thackeray, after returning from dining out and before dressing for bed, suffered a massive stroke. He was found dead on his bed the following morning. He was only fifty-two.

His death was entirely unexpected, and shocked family, friends and indeed the entire Nation.

It is said that at his funeral service thousands of mourners turned out to witness his passing. He was buried on December 29th at Kensal Green Cemetery, London.

William Makepeace Thackeray – A Concise Bibliography

The Yellowplush Papers (1837)
Catherine (1839–40)
A Shabby Genteel Story (1840)
Second Funeral of Napoleon (1841)
The Irish Sketchbook (1843)
The Luck of Barry Lyndon (1844)
Notes of a Journey from Cornhill to Grand Cairo (1846)
Mrs. Perkins's Ball (1846), under the name M. A. Titmarsh
Stray Papers: Being Stories, Reviews, Verses, and Sketches (1821-1847)
The Book of Snobs (1848)
Vanity Fair (1848)
Pendennis (1848–1850)
Rebecca and Rowena (1850)
The Paris Sketchbook (1840)
Men's Wives (1852)
The History of Henry Esmond (1852)
The English Humorists of the Eighteenth Century (1853)
The Newcomes (1855)
The Rose and the Ring (1855)
The Virginians (1857–1859)
Lovel the Widower (1860)
Four Georges (1860-1861)
The Adventures of Philip (1862)

Roundabout Papers (1863)
Denis Duval (1864)
The English Humorists of the eighteenth century: A Series of Six Lectures (1867)
Ballads (1869)
Burlesques (1869)
The Orphan of Pimlico (1876)

Thackeray wrote a numerous number of articles for magazines and the like as well as contributing many picture sketches to articles and his own books. Many were then collected and published together. We have listed his major works only for this bibliography.

www.ingramcontent.com/pod-product-compliance
Lightning Source LLC
Chambersburg PA
CBHW071343170626
46811CB00003B/959